To
Donna and

So pleased I get
to host you this time.

Thanks for coming!

Kate
Palmer

PROTEA
PRESS

YOU CAN SEE THE END OF THE WORLD FROM HERE

Kate Packman

PROTEA PRESS
www.proteapress.co.uk
First published by Protea Press in 2024

ISBN: 978-1-917506-04-5

Cover image and design by Charlotte Packman @charpackman_artanddesign

To find out more about our authors and books visit www.proteapress.co.uk.
Here you will find details of the support we offer to writers including events,
webinars and literary festivals. You can also follow us on:
Linkedin: Protea Press   X: @protea_press   Instagram: proteapressbooks

For Dad

The masts of a liberty ship, like little crosses
Mark the water, not far out to sea —
Fourteen hundred tonnes of high explosives.
Tucked in the belly of its liberty,

Snapped in half on the sands, beyond all help.

The truth of it — this wartime souvenir,
Is common knowledge. But whisper to yourself
That you can see the end of the world from here.

Ros Barber

(Found on the Sheerness Sea Defences, Isle of Sheppey)

41 Days

I scrunch my eyes closed, willing my son's words to disappear. My tears are heavy enough to wash the words off the page, but it won't make any difference. It's too late. There's no way I can forget I've read them.

Pulling my dad's cardigan tight around my shoulders, I sniff at the wool. I haven't washed it since he died and the smell of him comforts me. My shoulders heave again. *Deep breaths, Viv. Smell the soup; cool the soup.* I'd read that in a book once and the advice has stayed with me. It had made my therapist laugh but the funny side is lost on me tonight. More tears hit the page of my journal so before I lose the words, I dab at the salty puddle with my cardigan sleeve. The frayed wool stops the ink bleeding into the weave of the paper.

At my last therapy session my counsellor, Phil, suggested therapeutic writing might help control my symptoms and improve my mood. I'd told him about my old journals. *Re-*

reading past entries from when your life was more positive might help you gain perspective, Vivian.

'Well that back-fired, didn't it Phil?'

My curated collection of journals line my bookshelf on the landing. I had followed Phil's instructions and looked for something to re-read. Disregarding my childhood scribblings, buried in the loft space with my teenage journals and my geography A-level coursework (I can't bring myself to throw out the curled pages of my coastal erosion project), I searched through the ones I'd written in the last eleven years. I'd skipped past the one when I was pregnant (while carrying Jake I didn't blossom or bloom or any of the things people promise you) and pushed the most recent one, which was all about Dave, aside. The journal had to feature Jake though. Only Jake matters now.

Why did it have to be *that* journal I reopened?

I cover Jake's words with my fingers.

We'd been sat around the caravan table; the Spanish spring weather having let us down for the second day in a row. With a game of Happy Families underway, I quizzed our six-year-old son about what he wanted to be when he grew up. A baker? A police officer? A pilot? He hadn't hesitated to answer.

It doesn't matter, Mum. I'm only going to live 'til I'm twelve.

Dave laughed at Jake's morbid prophecy. Fear struck me like a slap across the face. Later that night, I wrote down his words, verbatim. If only I'd laughed too.

2

Jake's prophecy travels through my fingertips and scores itself into my mind with the permanence of a stonemason marking a grave. I close my journal and place it in my pocket. Pulling the cardigan tighter, I try to remember what my dad's hugs felt like.

While I relive Jake's words, my mum and son are in bed with their bellies full of greasy fish and chips. *Grandma's treat*, she cooed, *it'll be a while until we get to share a Sunday night takeaway again*. I tried to tempt my small family unit with Chinese food but I'd been outnumbered. I file the out of date takeaway menu back on the kitchen side, setting it between a letter pleading with me to insure my water pipes and a rather early invitation from Saga to subscribe to old age. Rude. I catch sight of Jake's school trip letter. Over dinner he had shown his grandma the itinerary for his residential visit to Normandy. It means he will be in France for his birthday. I pull the letter towards me. An official-looking A4 envelope, thick and high-quality compared to the school photocopy, comes with it. I push it away.

On bright summer days, we stand on our beach and squint at the smudge in the distance. It's probably Margate but when Jake was little we pretended it was France. When I imagine him there alone, it could be 20,000 leagues under the sea, not twenty odd miles across the Channel. Scout camp next week - on the island - feels doable, but France? My chest tightens and the tears restart. I won't be able to protect him in France and he's twelve in forty-one days.

Forty-one days.

It's only forty-one days 'til my birthday! Jake's innocent countdown at breakfast had sounded as ominous as the sunken munitions deep inside *SS Richard Montgomery*. A ticking bomb. Mum's disapproval rings in my ears. *I've no idea why you continue to live so near the coast and that ship.* She'd never understood my connection to the sea. Not that it would make any difference where we were on the island if that lot exploded. Folding the itinerary, I use it to bury my divorce papers, shoving them both into my unruly filing system.

01:49

Creeping onto the landing, I pause and listen for my mum's deep, nasal snoring. It's so unladylike that I can never bring myself to tell her how bad it sounds. I hope the cabin on her cruise ship has thick walls, or that the passengers are as deaf as her. I sympathise with other insomniacs. Through Jake's open door, I can see the shadow of his hand dangling over the side of his bed, his solar system duvet barely covering him. I must update his bedding to something more age-appropriate soon, though it will have to wait until I'm back at work on full pay.

The few family I have left sleep soundly, making me jealous.

4

Mum's snores rumble in time with the rolling waves lapping at the base of Minster cliffs. My room, without Dave keeping the bed warm, looks uninviting. Empty. The beach will be empty too. Better to wander an unspoilt coastline than toss and turn in bed. I tuck the greying strands of my unruly bob, too many to yank out now, behind my ears, and grab my navy coat off the banister to go over my Dad's cardigan.

02:19

The shingle tries to swallow my feet as small waves lap at the strandline. The earlier high tide mark, littered with tangled bladderwrack and the odd mermaid's purse, catches the moonlight. I walk along its edge. My mum used to moan at my untidy collection of dogfish cases. When I lived at home, the bathroom windowsill was littered with ocean detritus: rows of razor shells, crabs' discarded claws and one starfish (all appendages intact). The starfish now hangs on my bathroom wall between the dangly light pull and the mirror bordered with shell fragments. Dave had bought the mirror for me at the Shellness craft fair. He'd seen me fall in love with it and then walk away because of the price tag. He'd crept back, bought it and surprised me later that night by pulling it from under my pillow like a magician. Pebbles and pieces of driftwood — anything shaped by the sea's fists — still catch my eye, but I let

Jake do the cataloguing and displaying these days. My own ambitions of being a marine biologist are long buried.

I drag my shoe through the shingle, making a deep groove to match the lines that furrow my brow. I stretch out my forehead trying to smooth the lines away. I check the time: 02:30. My mum leaves for her cruise in a few hours. Two months around the Med. Sixty days.

She won't be here if it happens.

I'm glad she spent her last night on the island with us. I know it's her way of checking up on me but it also meant she saw her grandson one last time before his birthday. Jake had spent all evening grilling her for details of this 'once in a lifetime' trip. *The ship will be full, Jakey. I'll be able to wander out of my cabin, day or night, and there'll be someone on deck, or in one of the restaurants. There's every nationality of food. French delicacies one night, Thai the next. There's even a cinema on board!* Jake's eyes had widened at the thought of twenty-four-hour restaurants and free movies. He had speculated he might be eating croissants in France at the same time as she would be eating them on board her cruise ship. I should let him go to France. In the distance, the lights from a ship draw my attention to the horizon. My shoulders quiver as I shake off the thought of Jake crossing the sea without me.

Of him being trapped on a ferry with crowds of people.

Of him not being able to escape.

Crowds are becoming a problem for me. The more time I spend off work, the fewer people I see, the less I want company. Last night, my mum had teased me, *You're like a hermit. A hermit crab hiding in your house, and crotchety too.* She had snorted at her little joke and elbowed Jake in the ribs. I didn't laugh: her jibe stung. When dad had died, she retreated inward. Dave hadn't died; he'd left. But both equalled loss. Both hurt. I miss my dad more than Dave. I pull at his cardigan under my coat — folding myself between the swathes of wool that had been needed to reach around his expansive waistline. I'm still too angry with Dave to miss him.

Thought about going back to work, have you Vivian? Subtle as a sea wall my mum.

A ringed plover scuttles past, flashing black and white feathers as it splashes through the water's edge. It stops to wade the shallows and search for worms. I check my watch again, the cracked face reminding me of another expense I can't afford.

I had tried returning to work.

Humiliation flushes my cheeks. I rub my hands across my face, reshaping the skin to erase the shame. On the first day back after the summer break, I'd sat at one of the school desks, listening to a group of pupils share their holiday experiences. The teacher had hoped the new initiative of talking through their ideas before writing might help them put words on the page. My knees skimmed the underneath of the table. The pupils' pencil cases gleamed with the potential of a new school year. One of the pupils held everyone's attention as he announced his parents were getting a divorce. He had boasted about getting two holidays, described his two bedrooms, but I could see the pain behind his eyes. I tried to keep my emotions in check but the way his voice cracked, it broke me. Full sobs and angry tears had scourged my face. The pupils stared, mouths hanging open as I ran to the bathroom, mortified.

Obviously my mum thought I should try again. I had shut her down with a dark look and tucked back into the fish and chip supper I didn't even want. I won't discuss my anxieties in front of Jake. He's seen enough of my breakdown and heard enough about his dad being to blame.

Work, and Dave's absence, seem the least of my problems now. The scrawled words in my journal weigh me down like the stones Jake collects from the beach, bulging in my pockets until the fabric of my cardigan stretches, changing shape until they resemble monstrous growths. Tonight, I considered telling my mum about Jake's morbid prophecy, but when they both went to bed at the same time, my mum announcing *I need my beauty sleep*, the moment never arrived. The words, like the fossils on Warden Point beach, stay buried inside me.

It's better I don't tell her.

Worrying about me and Jake will spoil my mum's longed-for

holiday. The first holiday she has been brave enough to go on alone. And although I know a flippant dismissal of six-year-old Jake's words will follow my confession, my mum will nevertheless worry. She won't understand my fear. She won't acknowledge it. Phil's plea for me to *talk more, Vivian* does not apply here. My mum needs me to be okay, so she can enjoy herself. Have I managed to hide my escalating insomnia? Hanging around on the beach in the early hours of the morning might not help my case. I must get back before they wake.

I run my fingers through my hair. It needed a wash before and now salt tangles the strands together. Lack of sleep pulls at my face. Will my eyes betray me? Will each burst blood vessel reveal another broken night? As I climb the cliff path, passing the sea lavender and the pink daisies of the sea asters, I pinch my cheeks for colour. I will blame my red eyes on the early morning walk, a result of the sea spray and the sharp breeze coming off the water.

Once my mum leaves the island and boards the train for Southampton, I can relax again. Stop pretending I'm okay. Jake won't ask any questions. He doesn't want to know about my problems. A bit more time and my group therapy sessions will help. I shake out my limbs and start to head home. Once I can put the journal entry behind me, once I can convince myself not to believe six-year-old Jake and his dark prophecy, I will sleep better.

40 Days

01:34

On the boat and ready to depart. Ships ahoy!! Love you darling xx.

I close my mum's message from earlier and toss my face wipes to one side. Removing my pathetic amount of make-up requires too much effort so I collapse on top of my duvet instead. My mum's parting words at the train station, *Get some sleep*, stayed with me all day. I hadn't hidden my insomnia as well as I thought I had. Reaching out, I sweep my hand under my pillow and pull out my journal. I hold it to my chest. The pendant lamp swings above me, left to right in a steady rhythm. Does it fit the minimalist theme I attempted after reading *Hygge: The Danish Secrets of Happiness*, or is it plain and boring? Another failed attempt at making my room a sanctuary? When we had decorated, I chose the floral wallpaper on the feature wall behind the headboard for me and the large antique world map to please Dave. He used to trail his fingers, following the latitudinal lines across the map, gliding over the oceans. *Viv, I have spent all my life laying bricks and moving earth, I want to feel the waves beneath me next.* He made it sound so romantic. I let myself dream of studying marine life in my retirement. The expanding oceans and islands on his map now make me feel insignificant. How, at 51, have I not found my place in the world? *Try to focus on the space around you,* Phil's advice in our group sessions sounds helpful. I stroke my textured quilt. *You can't heal the world, only yourselves.* I have tried but my comfortable and cosy Scandinavian room fails to work on my stubborn mind. It refuses to relax.

It wants to stay awake.

To keep Jake safe.

The journal digs into my ribs. I release my grip and blink into the darkness. The light from the landing makes my eyes scrunch shut again. I battle it by opening them as wide as I can. My eyeballs sting with fatigue. I slow my blinking and link it to my breaths, conscious of the weight of each of my limbs as they sink into the mattress. A mattress I spent a small fortune on because it promised a perfect night's sleep. The anger at being ripped off reignites inside me. I shoo it away and push the negative energy into my legs instead, trying to visualise them as weighty lumps of lead. Like molten metal each limb melds together, down from my calves, to my ankles. I force my lump of a body into the mattress. Pushing downwards. Or should I be pulling downwards?

What did my yoga teacher say?

I've no idea. When did I last go to yoga? Even with my slow rhythmic blinking, my eyes refuse to stay closed. A car passes on the street outside. Someone finishing a night shift? A drunk driver? Hugh from across the road? The newly retired Malcolm next door? The pendant lamp swings again, a fraction to the left, and then re-centres itself. I regulate my breathing. *Smell the soup; cool the soup.* In through my nose and out through my mouth. Eyes shut. Jaw clenched. Pain pinches at my gums. Another deep breath.

Relax, Vivian.

The night jumbles my thoughts, and makes them swell and surge through my head. With the sound of another passing car, my eyelids pop back open. Saliva has accumulated in my mouth. I swallow. Fully awake again now.

I turn over and slide inside the covers.

01:57

A sliver of moon peeks past a cloud and illuminates the edge of my windowsill. The breeze entering the open window carries in the damp, briny scent of the North Sea. I want to go back to the beach but with mum gone there will be no more night

wanderings for a while. The open blind flaps in its casing. I try
to rub away a crop of goose-bumps gathering on my upper
body. The pool of sweat under my breasts and the dampness
between my thighs makes the chill more pronounced. I pull my
feet up and clasp my ankles, making myself as small as
possible. Impenetrable. Gathering the duvet over my face, my
warm breath raises the temperature of my skin a fraction. I
allow my eyesight to blur at the edges, like looking through the
dimpled frost of obscured glass. Itching my left eyelid, I smudge
the eyeliner I should have removed earlier. Sleep feels close
now. I let my eyelids fall and try to release the tension in my
muscles.

Clank!

The radiator? Or someone climbing the side gate?

Could be our cat, Smudge, leaping onto the fence.

I sit up. Swinging my legs round, I let them dangle over the
side of my bed. I stare out the window into the black street.
Pulling the cuffs of my pyjama bottoms down from mid-shin to
my ankles, I rub at the imprint the tight elastic has left on my
dry skin. Leg dandruff falls like dust motes, every flake
illuminated in the sudden blast of next door's security light. I
lean forward and peer further out. Darkness and shadows fill
my garden. They fight for space with the pools of yellow light
designed to deter intruders. Weeds sprout between cracks in
the unadopted road's decaying tarmac. As the security light

extinguishes, the moonlight reveals a scuffed circle of grass. A scar left by Jake's homemade goal.

02:03

Six minutes since I last looked. Six hours could have passed and I would still be awake. The dent in my pillow, shaped by my head, looks welcoming. The other side remains undisturbed. At least my insomnia only affects me.

I can hear Jake's pig-like snuffle through the thin dividing wall along with a bang on the plasterboard as he kicks out in his sleep. Dreaming of a winning goal. Maybe the noise came from him, not the radiator or the gate or the cat. We had constructed his bed into the corner of his room to maximise his Lego building space, not realising that his bed against the wall would mean every noise would travel through to our room. No. *My* room. He now fills the extra space with dirty socks, Nike joggers and discarded school work. Senior school pushed the boy out of him so quickly I missed it. In contrast, my room doesn't have an item out of place. Tidy room equals tidy mind. Another bit of advice I followed as if it were a religion. To no avail.

I push the digital display so it faces away from me, telling myself if I can feign sleep, it will come. I roll over and see Smudge sat like a sphinx on the bit of floor that houses the hot water pipes. The noise wasn't him. I go deeper under the covers, moving onto my front and re-positioning my breasts. Although they've shrunk since my thirties, they still manage to feel like forgotten wheat bags, cold and lumpy underneath me. I pull my vest straight to keep them from slinking out of the gaping jersey.

I grab my phone and tap at the Amazon Music app. Selecting the *Hamilton* soundtrack, I plug in my earbuds and play Eliza's *Helpless* number. The lyrics, rhythmic and soulful, give me something to focus on other than the place where my mind always wants to go at this time of night. My fingers reach out for my journal, now back under my pillow. I make myself pull away from the toxic pages.

I flip over and push my lower spine into the mattress, digging my heels in. Is it too firm? Should I buy a memory foam topper to cushion my increasingly heavy limbs? I check Amazon's Choice on my phone, but stop when I remember Phil's warnings of blue light curtailing my melatonin production, though not before I have received a notification of my paltry step count for the day. Tomorrow I will be more active. If I can exhaust my body, then it will be unable to resist sleep.

If only being exhausted was the solution to my problem. I manoeuvre on to my side to relieve the ache now creeping into my right hip. It's always my right hip. I wish my hip was the real problem.

My overactive mind is the problem. My head is the problem.

02:57

I wave my arms and legs around, hitting the abyss of cool cotton, like a snow angel exploring the empty space next to me. Cool and almost damp. The menopause broke my thermostat months ago and getting my temperature right remains a constant battle. I ruffle my summer quilt and hold armfuls of its crinkly cotton to my chest. I shouldn't need the extra winter layer for at least another month or two but without Dave, and the hot flushes that never come when I need them, I may have to dig it out of the loft sooner. Another one of Dave's jobs that now belongs to me.

I smooth out my hair. Bed head hair at fifty-one can be pulled off if you're Jenny Eclair but not if you're Vivian Farrington. Single mother. Pathetic. Failing at life. I need to get back to work but with no emotional capacity for the pupils, I can't face it. Yet without work, who am I? Not a wife. A mother.

And what if I didn't have Jake? My whole body shudders and I try to hold still against the shock of the possibility of not being Jake's mum anymore. Who will I be if the worst happens?

I move my hand down from the nape of my neck, over my breasts (still inside the vest) and past the sweaty damp patch, until I reach my middle. I stop at my waist, not quite love handles but definitely doughier than I would like. My palm sits at the top of my bikini line. I reach a little further, foraging for comfort. Would an orgasm help me relax? Help me sleep? No, any stimulation now would keep me awake even longer and I'd have to get out of bed to fetch my lube from the bathroom cabinet. Too much effort. Jake rolls over again, definitely his knee knocking the wall this time. Enough to send a tremor through the thin walls of our semi.

40 days until his birthday.

Jake's main concern is which pair of *fresh treads*, Nike obviously, my meagre bank account will cover. He might not understand why I cannot cope without Dave, as he acts fine without me, but he has been astute enough not to ask for a birthday party. His thoughtfulness makes me sad. He's *Killing Me Softly*. Another song I obsessed over, long before the *Hamilton* soundtrack. I start a new Amazon Music search on my phone.

I pull the journal out from under my pillow. Barcelona curls across the front in my best handwriting, along with the date: nearly six years ago. As a teenager, my journals held cinema tickets and bus timetables, favourite sweet wrappers, details of who loved who, and the experimental signatures of potential new surnames as if the boys at school were going to be future husbands. A map of my teenage neurosis. Every journal since Jake documents his last eleven years. All my moments revolving around him. I find the turned over corner and trace the fear of my scrawled handwriting with my fingertips. His words still frighten me. I snap it closed. Chuck it across the room. It slides over the worn carpet, missing Smudge by an inch and stopping at the skirting board. He glares at me and then turns to the journal. I follow his gaze and see the folded page.

The track restarts. I pull out my earbuds and shuffle down the bed. I push my fingers into my ears to relieve the pulsing ache, and turn over again.

39 Days

00.15

Meditating rarely works but I am putting in extra effort tonight. My rhythmic breathing starts its trick on each muscle and as it reaches my bum, my heavy limbs remind me of the epidural I needed for Jake. Two weeks overdue and with no signs of him making an appearance, the midwife induced my labour. The epidural didn't ease the birthing process. Once they discovered the baby in a back-to-back position, they wanted me on all fours. So uncouth, and impossible with paralysed limbs from the waist down. The final obstacle in an already exhausting pregnancy that led to an emergency c-section, followed by an array of stretch marks, grey hairs and dark circles under my eyes, that no amount of Touche Eclat (or the supermarket version anyway) can cover. Tonight I cleaned my teeth with the light off to avoid staring at my ageing face.

To be honest, my whole pregnancy had been riddled with bad omens. From the first day of my second trimester, morning sickness struck. The nausea pestered me day and night until the twentieth week. Any hint of a banana or a whiff of tuna triggered an attack in milliseconds, making my lunch breaks at work challenging. Only McVitie's Ginger Nuts and Walkers Cheese and Onion crisps settled my churning stomach, much to my desk neighbour's disgust. I worked in the shipping office then. The best thing was the view of the sea.

I must remember to tell the Scout leader at camp next week that Jake won't eat tuna.

The morning sickness set the tone for the whole pregnancy. As the nausea abated, heartburn made its debut. Sitting at any angle less than ninety degrees made acid bubble to the top of my throat like an erupting volcano. Excessive pregnancy hormones slackened the valve that kept my stomach acid safely in situ. Combine those symptoms with my elephantine bump (everyone's 'oh I thought you were further along' exclamations haunted my final trimester) and sleep was elusive then too.

It had been the sixteen week blood test that initiated me into the world of parental worry. And it continued long after the midwife placed my healthy baby boy in my arms. Clumsy accidents, raging temperatures and unexplained symptoms – were they all signs that something was wrong even then? Pre-pregnancy must have been the last time I slept well, although if I can keep this heavy sensation going, I might get all the way to my head and sleep tonight.

Pins and needles prickle my right buttock first. The heaviness starts to recede. *Damn*. Rarely does the meditation trick get past my waist, so I was kidding myself tonight would be any different. The wind outside isn't helping either. The super skinny weather lady (and they say the camera adds 10lbs) predicted the Indian summer days we had been enjoying earlier in the week would soon be replaced by high winds. All part of island life. It sounds like the winds have already arrived. The yellow exclamation mark on my weather app this afternoon warned me of the dangers. Next door's boundary of conifers warn me now. The wind travelling through them speaks in ominous rumbles, like thunder's cousin.

As does everything since I re-read that journal entry.

I'm only going to live 'til I'm 12.

Pain shoots through my clenched jaw. *Try to relax your muscles, Vivian.* Easy for Phil to say. *Try a warm, milky drink.* Mum's advice always sounded like something from a 1950's domestic science manual.

Before she left for her holiday, she pointed out Jake's milky white ankles. Bony and pale, they peeked out of his pyjama bottoms. A part of him which was always hidden from the sun by his preference for long socks. He refuses to wear trainer socks, even Nike ones. *They're annoying, Mum. They fall down. Anyway, who cares if I have white ankles?* My mum shook Jake's shoulders. *You're growing up too fast, love. Promise not*

21

to grow another inch while I'm on my cruise! But if he doesn't grow up...my mum's plea sounds like a curse.

Thank God Jake has no memory of his words that Easter holiday. Not that I believe in God but I am keeping my options open. Jake talks about his future. He longs to be older – to be 15 so he can watch some violent film or join in some inappropriate video game that I have censored. I refuse to pander to his ranting about the unfairness of it all. He talks as if everything ahead of him is guaranteed. As he should. Why do I believe what he said in Spain? If he had said he was going to be an astronaut, I would have smiled and nodded in agreement, knowing full well his dreams were just that. Why do I insist on treating these words as a sign? I can hear how ludicrous trusting my gut sounds but that's the truth of it. Like some genetic code, inherited from my ancestors, something inside me tells me to believe him.

Earlier, due to the humidity of the day and the fluctuating temperatures of menopause, I left my windows open but the gusts of wind are bypassing my stuffy semi tonight. The melody of my wind chime clashes with the gentler tone of Malcolm's wooden version. His deep hollowness accompanied by my tinkling metal. The room falls into silence for brief moments, until disrupted by the uproarious whirls of wind whipping at the leaves that cling to the branches as they try to make it to the end of summer. The gale outside fights with the soundtrack of the waves on the beach as it pushes and pulls the air. My bedroom door taps in its frame. Another repetitive noise to keep me awake.

02:26

I get up to close the door, but stop midway. If I close it, I won't hear Jake if he gets up in the night. Before I make it back into bed, a wind more suited to the plains of Neptune catches the door. Until Jake told me his random science fact of the week this morning, I had no idea other planets had winds. The door slams shut.

I pause, listening in case Jake stirs.

Nothing. Not a murmur. Not even a whimpered word. It has been months since I heard him sleep talking. I miss his random instructions. *Don't put onions in it. No, Mum. No.* Such an honour to walk through his dreams.

I go back, reopen the door and close the window instead.

Puffing up the pillows, both sides, I climb back in, knowing it won't make any difference to my comfort. Lying down, my neck supported by one of Dave's pillows, I let my eyes track the line of cracked paint on the ceiling. I stop when it reaches the coving. I close my eyes and hold myself still. My arms clamped to my sides. I must resemble a body at a wake. Every holiday Jake always pleaded with Dave to bury him in the sand. The weight of the beach holding him down. I shake off the thought of Jake being buried alive. My eyes flick open.

The wind continues its battle with the trees, turning itself inside out. Buffeting and hissing through the chimney and vented bricks. Throwing the covers off to release some of my newly accumulating heat, the peg bag on the washing line rattles as it attacks our discarded barbeque. Jake keeps asking to use it. *Dad isn't here, Mum, and I thought you told me that women can do anything men can do. So why can't we have barbequed burgers?* Trying to goad me into action with my own feminist rant. *Because, Jake, it's messy and I will have to cook and clean the thing too.* I cringe at my pathetic excuse. Have I deprived him of his last barbeque? The wind tells me that autumn's clawing at the edge of summer so I probably have.

38 Days

01:51

I scroll through my messages. No more updates from my mum. Perhaps she isn't as worried about me as I thought. I put the phone face down on the bedside table and look at sheep jumping over gates, as they travel up my arm and across my chest. It's been a while since I played games to entice sleep but these new pyjamas encourage me. Despite them being a relatively expensive garment (not that I paid full price, a charity shop find) there appears to have been no attempt to pattern match the front and rear. Why do Patrick and Esme, on *The Great British Sewing Bee*, expect such high standards from competitors, when Boden appear unperturbed by decapitated sheep? Should I count the sheep that disappear into the seam as one, none or half? Half would stimulate my brain more. But to ignore them feels like cheating. I settle on counting them — they are there after all. Every time I get to the faux buttons across the middle, I lose count. After a third attempt, I abandon the task. It's not working.

I tip onto my front, with a pillow under my raised knee to ease my niggly right hip. The red digital clock display taunts me. We will be up at six for school and that leaves four hours if I fall asleep right now. No such luck.

I should get up. I could watch the twenty-four-hour news channel. On the earlier bulletin there had been a court case reporting the sentencing of a truck driver who had killed a father and son. I change my mind. Stories repeat hourly and I cannot face seeing the weeping mother stood on the court house steps again. Widowed and childless. What is the word for when your only child dies? Is there a word? Are you even a mother any more?

In weeks, days, hours that could be me.

Would it be easier if I knew when?

If I knew, I could try to outwit the prophecy. Move house (even if that meant negotiating with Dave). Go somewhere or do something outlandish, unpredictable. Do something I would never have imagined myself doing to try and bend fate.

Fate. I wish I didn't believe in it.

Jake's words were assured. His tone certain enough for me to record it in my journal, but his morbid statement had not perturbed him. In the daylight, I can dismiss his childish words, like all his weird and incessant questions and observations at that age. *What's your favourite room in the house? Do flies drink? What coin do you like the best? 2op is my favourite.* But at night, as the clouds look like dark shadows of their former daytime selves, these words become a prophecy that will come true no matter what I do to prevent it.

02:29

A niggle in my abdomen suggests I might need to pee – I should try.

I stop at Jake's door on the way to the bathroom. Pausing for a moment, I pick at the sticky residue of an old nameplate. Matthew. A memory of the house's previous owners creeps into my head. Their son and his quiet, solemn demeanour that had unsettled me when we viewed the house. He had watched our every move, glaring at us as we admired his tidy room. Yellowing gloss paint, which could do with a refresh, and that sticky mark, gather dust and hair in the shape of his name. I stop picking at it in case I eradicate him. I shake my head. I cannot think about Matthew now. Jake's room will always remain partly his.

I poke my head through the doorway. The light from the hall falls onto Jake's discarded clothes. A swirling whirlpool in the middle of his floor. His knees have created a tent in the covers; his favourite teddy sits tucked in the gap next to him. Not too old for teddy. His bone structure, accentuated by the night shadows, reveals his jaw pushing through the skin, reshaping his boyish thickness into a chiselled chin. Up and out. Up and out. The pattern of his growth spurts, like the peaks and troughs of an ECG. Earlier we visited the barbers and I can see a line of pale skin glowing like a halo around his scalp, where it's been starved of the sun. Without Dave to do the barber visit we'd left it longer than usual. I want to stroke his nose in the way I did when I settled him in his cot after a midnight feed. My fingers reach for the fringe he asked the barber to keep long. It hangs across his forehead, kissing his lashes. Sleeping seems like sacrilege when I could be watching Jake. What if we only have 38 days? That's no time at all. I admire his gingery freckles. My eyes connect all the dots gathered on his nose and cheeks. I reach a large mole on his neck. My fingers reach out but he turns away before I can get there. Has it grown? It looks darker. I'll check more closely tomorrow.

Backing into the hallway, I manage to step on the exact spot that creaks like the splitting *Titanic*. I hold my breath, motionless on the guilty spot of floor, and watch Jake's knees as his duvet tent collapses. He resettles and I continue to the bathroom.

After my evening bath (with lavender oil — another unsuccessful remedy that I won't give up on), I had opened the window, pushing it to its limits. I pull it to now, and then wiggle on to the toilet. The winds from yesterday shook loose

28

most of the leaves from my sycamore tree, and with no Dave to do the annual topping, I will have a larger pile than usual to rake up when I can face the garden chores. Maybe I should ask Jake to help, although he'd probably demand pocket money that my finances won't stretch to. It's the warm, wet summer's fault, giving the tree an extra growth spurt. A tree surgeon I approached had wanted an astronomical amount to do Dave's job so on a windy day like yesterday its unruly top threatens the fence, and then litters my lawn with its waste.

Tonight's still air makes the high winds of yesterday a distant memory. Living on the east coast, I witness the seasons overlap every year and now the humidity of summer is back, and curtailing my breathing with its heavy air. I pull my pyjama bottoms back up and replace the toilet seat. When Jake was a baby, I moved through the house trying not to wake him. Now I will him to move. To make sounds of life. I check on him again on the way past, though avoiding the creaky board this time. He sleeps in the way I long to. Lights out, eyes closed. So simple.

I collect my journal from under my pillow. The butterflies in mid-flight hustle for space across the cover and curve around the spine. I slip it beneath my arm. With the chance of sleep distant, I take the journal and head to the kitchen for a milky drink. As I pass the bookshelf on the landing where my other journals live, I even out the space between 2015 and 2017.

Hiding its absence. Once in the kitchen, I slide my paperwork to one side and place my journal on the work surface. Laying my hand on the cover, I brace myself as a shudder of fear travels down my spine. The turned-down corner marks the page but I ignore it, even though I had brought it downstairs to read. To manipulate those words. To reassure myself that I can re-interpret his premonition and solve my incessant insomnia. Why do I give those words so much might? Enough to tear through my life like a juggernaut. Jake planned to be a farmer, then a barber, and for a brief time, an alien invader. He had begged to take home the 103-year-old tortoise named Henry who had charmed us at Barcelona Zoo, because it would help him to become a vet. None of those words had the power of prophecy. Kids make no sense.

Nonsense.

Kids talk nonsense.

My gut refuses to agree. And I trust it. Know it knows. It knew when my mum came to my house to tell me about dad's accident. It knew when Dave didn't come home that night. I would never claim to be psychic but I know to believe in gut instinct. However it works, it knew when I wanted, with all my might, to leave the waiting room and decline the routine second trimester blood test.

Twelve years later, the same sensation tells me to listen. I can't ignore it even if I want to.

The room had been full of people, all clinging onto their request slips, all silent and wriggling in the uncomfortable waiting room chairs. Sixteen weeks pregnant, I held my non-existent bump. Only my mum and best friend had noticed and that was due to my burgeoning breasts, not my waistline. I touch what is left of them, and a tingle of pleasure travels down my abdomen despite their emptiness.

All I wanted to do was walk out of that waiting room.

The desire to leave came from deep inside my body. The place I imagined the seed of my baby had rooted itself to me. If I abandoned my place in the queue, I could pass my numbered ticket on to some lucky patient so they could escape the hospital a little quicker. Instead I reasoned with myself. I labelled my irrational fear hormonal, coming from a place in my head I could not control. A place that continues to imagine every worst-case scenario without my permission. That day I searched my head and it gave me no rational reason to leave, so I chatted to the nurse as she extracted my blood, making small talk about holiday destinations and the footfall through the hospital that day. Our conversation punctuated with well-practised instructions.

There will be a small prick. There we go. All done now. Hold this here. Keep the pressure nice and firm. There may be a slight bruise. Nothing to worry about.

I held the puff of cotton wool in place. Trying to keep the

worry inside me.

I had been right. There was something to worry about. The blood test revealed a one in seventy-seven chance of delivering a Down syndrome child. At nearly forty, I had known this unexpected pregnancy might bring problems with it. The unflattering label, geriatric mum, plastered all over my paperwork on my first appointment left me in no doubt. But, as my first, and likely to be, only child, it did not seem too greedy to expect a healthy one. (I tried to forget the mistake in my twenties that never made it to full term, *For the best* mum said. And the guilt that went along with it.)

The blood test results had meant decisions had to be made.

Dave had left them up to me. That should have rung an alarm bell.

Should we have an amniocentesis to find out if we would be taking on a child for the rest of our adult lives? If we were, should we keep it? A child we were likely to leave behind helpless. Or worse still, outlive. Dave had not wanted a disabled child — he made that clear. *But Viv, it's your choice. You're the one who's pregnant.* He had never said he wouldn't help but implicitly I knew, if worst came to worst, I would be doing it alone. However, living in ignorance until the baby arrived had felt equally unbearable.

The amniocentesis needle loomed over me. I closed my eyes to its length and held my breath. Dave held my hand and looked away. The thought of another miscarriage locked my eyelids shut as the doctor inserted the needle and the nurse pushed cold jelly over my swollen waist with the ultrasound wand, monitoring our unborn child.

I rub my stomach where the needle punctured my womb. Trace my finger across the silvery line of my c-section scar.

There had been no sign of abnormalities. All that risk for a few reassuring words. *A healthy baby boy.* Were they wrong after all? Were there abnormalities that they couldn't see on the scan back then? Could there be something genetically wrong with him that will strike before he's twelve?

I stir a little boiling water into my cocoa mug, trying to squish any pockets of powder. Leaning back against the kitchen counter, I keep watch to make sure the milk doesn't boil over. My broken microwave gathers dust in the corner. I should look on Facebook Marketplace for a second hand one. My fingers are drawn back to my journal, tracing a butterfly's wing. My chewed nail creeps under the folded corner to lift the page. I flick it over. Tear stains bloom like grey clouds.

My eyes reach the words at the same time as the milk erupts. I dash to the stove and pour the frothing milk into my cocoa paste and whisk. It darkens to a rich chocolate colour. Despite my best efforts, bubbles of powder rise to the surface. I tip the scorched pan into the sink, emptying the remaining kettle water in to soak it and head up to bed with my mug, leaving my journal behind on the kitchen side.

37 Days

Jake's already snoring and Film4 deemed *Taken 3* worth
showing again so I am in bed earlier than usual. Maybe this will
help me relax. I miss Dave's Netflix account, but refuse to login
and use it even though he probably wouldn't notice.

I sit in bed, and pinch Dave's pillows to prop myself up.

No, scrap that. Both sets of pillows are mine.

Dave lost any entitlement to the pillows when he walked out.
When he took off with no warning, or when I am feeling fairer,
no specific warning. I stroke his side of the bed, flattening out
the creases in the sheets. His bedside table sits empty as I
remain uncomfortable commandeering it and the oily patch
from his hair product won't budge off the dove grey headboard
either. I try to stroke the pile of the velvet in the opposite
direction to disguise it but the stain persists. Everything
reminds me I once shared the room with him whether I want
to remember or not.

Viv. He said my name in a way no one else ever has. He made me sound fun. We'd been laid on top of the covers, complaining about the stuffy air after a warm day in May. We'd watched the sunset from the garden. He stroked my knee and let his hand trail towards my bikini line. My body pulsed for him but I still had an essay to finish for my Open University course. Dreams of being a science teacher were at least six modules and three years away. *Do you ever fancy spicing things up?*

Spicing what up? Dinners?

He sniggered. Offered a patronising eyebrow raise. *Err no, I meant in the,* he arced his hands outwards in a grand, theatrical way, *in the bedroom.*

Oh. I didn't rush to reply. Not sure if he meant with toys, or role-play or maybe a bit of porn. I'd seen his magazine wedged behind the bathroom cupboard. Well, I assumed it was his and not the previous owner's. *Do you mean dressing up or games or...what do you mean?*

Well, I was thinking of someone joining us.

The words hung over our bed like saturated clouds.

What?

Well, there's this gir...I mean, this woman from work, who suggested that we could all enjoy each other. I let him ramble on, too shocked at first to respond. We had married because of Jake but I thought things were okay. Good even. I shuffled up the bed. Clutching my A4 pad tighter and inching away until his hand slid off my knee. He continued. *You know I'd have sex with you and she'd watch or vice versa or we can all...*he stumbled over the next word...*play with each other.*

I know what a threesome is, Dave. And I'm not interested. Despite my cross tone, desire pulsed below my waist, my body betraying me and reaching for extra blood. I clenched my buttocks and ignored it.

Okay. Okay. He held up his hands in mock surrender. *I'm not bothered either way. Just thought I'd offer in case you were. No worries.* He blathered on. I went back to my essay and he turned off his lamp. Our marriage nose-dived from there. It officially sank when I came home from work and saw the house looking as if it belonged to someone else. *Wow, Dad tidied. What did he do?* I asked Jake, smirking at my own joke.

Eh?

Where's your dad? Did he tidy up?

Dunno. He's not home yet. My gut screamed at me that something was wrong. When did he tidy? The house hadn't looked tidy when I left that morning. I'd gone straight to yoga after work. Everything seemed roughly the same so I ignored my gut and started dinner. Sorted out Jake. Uniform off. Homework started. Walked him to and from Scouts. Weekday evenings are always so busy. When he didn't arrive home, I assumed he must be working late. Perhaps on a building site with no service as my texts bounced back. It took me until nine o'clock, once Jake was in bed and settled, to find the time to boil the kettle and sit down at the kitchen table. The note was there waiting for me, leant against my lemon and ginger teabags. Back when I still cared how much caffeine I consumed. His words were squeezed onto the back of an envelope from the Swale Borough Council about a rise in their rates.

He'd booked a day's holiday from work.

Packed all his belongings and left.

He wouldn't need to come back and disturb us as he'd been into the loft and retrieved his precious vinyl collection and lifted the carpets to remove the wires that connected his surround sound speakers to the TV. Music had left with him and the house quietened with only two of us to fill it.

I inspect the dents in the carpet where the five cinema-style speakers had sat. Poking at the squashed pile with my toes. I'd recently read, in some housekeeping magazine, whilst waiting to have my filling repaired, that placing an ice cube to melt on the dent would lift the pile. I must try that.

What he didn't do was say goodbye to me, or more significantly, to Jake.

I forced myself not to influence Jake's view of his father but inside I hoped his abandonment had manifested a grudge the size of Gibraltar Rock, where we spent our first family holiday, and I hoped it would be as immovable.

Like Jake's age. Eleven. The same number of journals on my
shelf. Jake asked about them over breakfast. As the kettle boiled,
his eyes settled on the butterflies covering my journal. Their
wings fluttering over the kitchen side. He reached for it.

How many have you got?

*Eleven of these. One for every year since I knew you were on
the way.* The boiling kettle roared as if it would erupt. I flicked
it off, keeping my eyes on Jake and the journal. *The teenage
editions are in the loft.*

*Did you know hot water can sometimes freeze faster than
cold water?*

No, I didn't. And I probably should have if I want to be a
science teacher.

It's called triple point. He picked up my journal off the
kitchen side and began to flick through the pages.

Do you still write every day?

Not at the minute.

Why not? I hadn't known what to say to that. How do you
tell your eleven year old son that your thoughts are so dark you
are scared to write them down?

Can I read it? My breath caught in my throat. *Not really.*

Why?

It's personal.

But it's only me.

Yeah but I'm not only your mum.

Eh?

Well, some things you don't talk about with your mum. Or your son.

What like?

*Lady stuff and…*I hesitated. I needed to make sure that he would never want to read them. He mustn't see those words. *I'm only going to live 'til I'm twelve.* And I couldn't resist the chance to embarrass him.

Sex Jake!

Eww, Mum. Jake pretended to vomit. *Anyway, Dad's moved out.*

The answer's no, Jake. End of.

The butterflies were still in his grasp. The folded corner marked the territory of my secret. I leant forward, determined not to snatch it. *Ta.* I held out my hand. Winced as I said the word I had promised myself, as a new mum, to never teach Jake. My son would say 'thank you' properly, not 'ta'. But as soon as all the other mums at Bumps and Babies started saying it, I had joined in. Along with using a baby voice, talking about bowel movements whilst eating, and sharing childbirth horror stories over artisan coffee. The clichés of motherdom.

He reluctantly handed it over.

I stare at the small top drawer of my bedside table where it now nestles between the commemorative five pound coin my mum gifted Jake for the Queen's Jubilee, a few misshapen kirby grips, an expired condom (ribbed for my pleasure), fungal nail treatment and a Tesco receipt for chicken thighs, milk and beard oil. I wish I'd bought Dave the value brand now.

I reach into the drawer and pull out the journal. It falls open on the page.

I fumble with my glasses until the writing comes into focus. I wish the words would crawl off the page and escape into the margins. Would he really die by his twelfth birthday? Is that what it means? Why at quarter to midnight did it seem so plausible?

I had a colleague once, who played with a Ouija board and somehow predicted she would be widowed and left alone with a small child. Her husband died aged thirty-four from a rare heart condition while she still nursed her son. Another friend always knew she'd have a starter husband. She was divorced after eighteen months.

What if Jake knew something I didn't?

23:51

Still not midnight. The oppressive air outside refuses to absorb the sound of the waves crashing on the shore tonight. A constant and dull thud smashes back and forth, as if Poseidon

41

sucks on the pebbles and spits them out. The North Sea swells and wanes less than a mile away. My home's elevated position, the bare fields and nothing more than the odd privet hedge and Malcolm's conifers stand between us and the sea so the noise travels unfettered through the midnight sky. At my yoga classes, the instructor plays ocean soundtracks to aid meditation, instead it relaxes the opening to my bladder, so I now have to pack an extra Tena Lady for each session. When had I last been to yoga? Weeks ago? Months?

I need to pee.

23.57

Maybe if I removed my Fitbit, I would not be as tempted to look at the time. Every hour it records my heart rate and the flash of neon green makes me take a peek at the screen. Although, if I removed it, my sleep patterns would not be recorded and I like to analyse the data over a morning coffee. Strong and black. I remember the perverse joy the first time I synced the watch with the app and discovered how little sleep I had achieved, the satisfaction of being right. Forty-three minutes of deep sleep. One hour fourteen minutes of light sleep. The rest of the witching hours, active. No wonder I resemble the walking dead.

Before being signed off work with stress, *home-related not work related* as the occupational therapist liked to point out each session, I compared sleep data with my colleagues during break times. Competed with is maybe more accurate. The person by the urn with the lowest average deep sleep recorded over the week always looked victorious. Winning for being the most fucked up. Two of my competitors had young children, so their sleep deprivation, being both temporary and duty-bound, was always usurped by my insomnia. Incurable and unmedicated. Mostly.

I collect the sleeping tablets from the bathroom cabinet. Never more than once a fortnight. I am strict about that. The clack of the child-locked bottle announces my failure with every squeeze. With the third twist, I pull off the lid and shake out two blue capsules. I toss them into my mouth and take them with the stewed dregs of my ginger tea, now the colour of my urine after a morning of black coffees. I must drink more water. I return my journal to the drawer and close my eyes while I wait for the drugs to work.

36 Days

The caffeine I consumed today to allay my drug-induced fog still screams its way through my bloodstream. My discarded mug from breakfast clutters the bedside table — an IKEA ceramic glass-style mug (a glug? a muss?). It holds double my standard coffee mugs. How many times had I refilled it today? My hand tremors. I put down my book next to the...glug. Rubbing my puffy eyes, I recognise the buzz trickling through my veins isn't going to wane any time soon. I know better than to drink coffee after lunch so tonight's insomnia serves me right.

Unless tonight's quivering hands can be attributed to shock. I shake them out but the tremors remain.

Jake had stirred, an hour after his bedtime. As his footsteps padded down the stairs, I waited for him to appear in the doorway before I demanded, *Get back to bed.* The sight of his pallid skin and the heave of his shoulders alarmed me. I stopped the snap in my voice and softened my tone.

Bad dream?

No.

What is it? His whole body shuddered.

Come here. I wrapped my arms around him. Grateful he still fit. *Come on, tell me. Mummy can... sorry, I mean, Mum can handle it.* I kept the pitch of my voice level and light, and stayed still. Perched on the edge of the sofa. I had paused Olivia Colman on the TV, posed pulling an unflattering face that made her chin look like it went straight down to her collarbone. Her character stationary and windswept on a beach in Dorset. Despite the unfortunate murder, I had liked the look of the place.

Come on. It can't be that bad.

Fat tears rolled down his cheeks. He stuttered over each word. My mind raced through possibilities. School? His PE teacher had always seemed over-familiar. And there was one of the Scout leaders, the one with bohemian hair and shoddy tattoos who never quite managed full eye contact. The *Broadchurch* storyline about a murdered boy flitted through my consciousness. What was parenting 101 for listening to accusations of abuse? I definitely had some safeguarding training at work about not asking leading questions, but inset days were so overfilled, the information so overwhelming, that my concentration often slipped. Something about not promising to keep their secrets. I stopped my speech mid-sentence. Tried to adjust my expectations in line with reality. *Don't catastrophise everything, especially without any evidence, Vivian.* Phil's words reminded me to slow down. To rein it in. A school bully, more likely.

Has someone done something to you?

My pulse raced. *Jake?*

No. I gripped his shoulders a little tighter.

Come on. Tell me. What is it?

Well, I have diarrhoea.

Oh, okay. Just now?

Yeah.

Okay.

And yesterday.

Oh well, don't worry — it's probably just the ready meal korma you had. Oh, crap. You ate the leftovers tonight — why didn't you say earlier? Before I gave you the leftovers?

Sorry. More fat tears fell. I pulled him in closer until my head rested on his chest. The beat of his heart tapped a rhythm on my face. His skin alive with heat, dampened my cheek.

You're burning up. His pulse raced with mine. *It's only diarrhoea, poppet. You'll be fine.*

It's not.

It's not what?

Just diarrhoea. Someone had done something. Had he had

PE today? My stomach lurched. Afraid to hear the answers, I
swallowed the rising bile.

I braced myself and squeezed his hand. He pulled away as I
crushed his fingers together. The bones gyrating in my grip. His
child-sized hand so vulnerable. He couldn't find the words. His
skin flushed. With embarrassment? Humiliation?

There was blood.

Blood? Oh. Alarm bells screamed in my ears. *How much
blood?*

A bit.

In your... poo? Sorry to be gross, but I need to know. I tried
hard to keep my face neutral as hospital rooms, surgeons,
deathbeds raced through my head.

No. When I wipe.

Okay. Just today?

And yesterday.

*Well, it's probably from wiping too hard. And the curry, you
know food poisoning can make you really sore.* His eyes
widened. Had someone hurt him? Is that why there was blood?
He looked petrified. Worse than when we had to be rescued
and escorted off the haunted house ride at Disney, part way
through the experience.

It's been like that since Norfolk.

What, in August?

Yes.

When you had the dodgy stomach? The strain to maintain my neutral expression compressed my muscles; I feigned rigor mortis to hide my fear. My breathing betrayed me. I could hear myself swallowing. The unexpected tropical heat of the holiday. Jake bodyboarding in the sea for four days straight. Our first holiday without Dave. Sun, sea and sand. On the fifth day of the holiday, the weather broke and a stomach bug struck Jake down during a pub meal. We ended the chalet holiday early and after two weeks, as I considered booking a doctor's appointment because Jake still couldn't digest his food normally, it cleared up. Or so I thought. We blamed the sea water. Salty and full of bacteria.

You've had blood in your bowel movements since Norfolk?

What are bowel movements?

Your poo.

Yes.

Why didn't you tell me?

Because I was embarrassed. It sounded like a confession. Sobs joined the fat tears.

Come here. I squeezed him. Encompassing him this time, stretching my eyelids wide until I could feel the sting.

All I could think about as I held him were the scrawled words in my journal.

Can I still go on the Scout trip? I nodded in agreement, ignoring the fear settling over me.

48

It took until ten o'clock to settle him. I fear nothing will settle me tonight.

I contemplate a make-up wipe wash or closing my eyes and shutting everything out. I choose the latter and lean back into the headboard. Jake will need to be off school for forty-eight hours. No, it's Saturday tomorrow so he will be able catch up on sleep and be ready for school on Monday, if he seems well enough. I have been practising what I will say to the doctor's receptionist. The arrogance I will need to convey to secure an appointment. I try to curtail the annoyance manifesting inside me already. Why aren't the doctors open over the weekend?

Yes, it is urgent. Blood in his stools. Stools sounds more medically-trained than hysterical parent. *Since August. It's over a month but he's only just told me. We would like to see a doctor. Today if possible.* I will remain polite. Stay calm, whether I am third or thirtieth in the queue. I set an alarm so I don't miss the phone line opening at eight o'clock.

23:47

One hour exactly. Stomach cramps twist my insides and I know the fear that was etched across Jake's brow causes my internal stabbing pains. I refrained Googling his symptoms earlier and watched the repeat of *Broadchurch* in a passive blur instead but still my body reacts. My 'sleepy' tea sits on the bedside table.

Untouched. Maybe I should have Googled it. I would then have the facts circulating my head rather than made up rubbish. *Catastrophising*, the doctor and my counsellor call it. The doctor put it on my sick note like I was being melodramatic and prescribed me with sleeping tablets and group sessions with Phil. In fact, if we are going to get anywhere with the doctors I need a list of questions for whoever we see; no doubt they will fob us off with a nurse practitioner. Doctors only see those who are dying. I will need to be direct and specific with my online search. What does it mean if my child bleeds from the bum?

Rectal bleeding is rare in children.

Crohn's disease.

IBS.

Colitis.

Nothing immediately life-threatening.

Isn't there an advert about not ignoring blood in bowel movements? Or does that only relate to middle-aged men? I know I shouldn't factor the diary entry into the diagnosis, but why had that come to my attention now and not five years from now? Or four? Or three? A warning? To take these symptoms seriously? Some higher power making sure, a month before his twelfth birthday that I know not to ignore these streaks of blood.

None of it explains why he is so scared. When did eleven-year-olds become so anxious about being sick? His crumpled face and wide eyes revealed his primal fear. Even if he does make out he is fine. Has he seen the adverts too? Exposure to all that reality TV? Maybe I shouldn't have watched *24 Hours in A&E* with him. Not that I normally let Jake watch it, it was a one-off. The world is a scary enough place. Jake's face told me he thinks it's serious.

My gut believes him.

Did my face expose me too? Does he know I think it's serious? I tried to smile, to push the worry away. *We'll ring the doctors on Monday and get you checked out.* Kept my tone light. *I'm sure it's nothing but we better get it checked. For peace of mind.*

I swallow my breaths until the air sticks in my chest and try to fight off the irrational fear stalking my subconscious by shaking out my limbs. I recognise the signs of an impending panic attack trying to break free. My thoughts crash into each other. Pound at my skull. My own blood test got it wrong. He hadn't had Downs.

Be reasonable, Vivian chimes Phil. *Say the words out loud. Banish them from your head.* I try.

'No child can know their date of death.' My voice evaporates in my empty room.

Google suggests this blood and diarrhoea is not life-threatening. The condition is likely to be an intolerance to one of the food groups.

Nothing more serious.

But there is a whole weekend until the surgery phone lines open. Unless this would class as an emergency? I will double-dial from my home phone and mobile to improve my chances of securing an appointment.

My eyes water with the effort of staying open, but when I close them, I see Matthew. The shy boy who didn't like us looking around his house with our eager eyes. His family had moved in with relatives because their new build wasn't ready for them and no one wanted to break the chain of sale. Within weeks, he had collapsed in their garden and when the diagnosis came, it was terminal. Within a year, he was gone. Malcolm next door had attended his funeral but wouldn't talk about it when he came back. I remember him walking his dog as usual in his black funeral suit. The darkness of it making the grey in his beard stand out. His polished shoes mottled with mud and sand shuffled on the broken paving slabs. It was as if all the life had been drained out of him. Did Jake remember? Did he hear me talking about it to Dave? Matthew was about twelve. It sounds like a rational explanation for Jake's prophecy. It feels like rare progress in the darkness.

Did his words in 2016 manifest themselves into this prophecy after he overheard me talking about that poor boy?

Jake had been three when we moved in. Could a boy so young, transpose that story onto his own future? His room remains the same pale blue. As if he shares the room with Matthew. Had the old owner visited the new one? Surely if any spirit would try to return, it would be a child. To ponder what he missed out on? What he might have become? Did he whisper into Jake's ears at night? Did he wish he was Jake?

The weight of my imagination pulls at my neck. My body sinks into the bed and I bury my face into the pillow. I can't close my eyes because every time I do, I see his hollow face. Why does my imagination insist on showing me what a dying twelve-year-old might look like?

23:56

Nine minutes pass at night like nine hours in the day. *Time is a manmade construct.* Dave loved to imagine he had vast scientific knowledge that made him impressive to others. Always spouting some fact or other. Facts most people wouldn't be able to refute. Jake still mimics him, not realising his random daily science facts feel like knives in my back. I was supposed to be the scientist. Not Dave.

00.27

Twenty-seven. The age I would have become a parent if things had worked out the first time. Would I have had Jake if I hadn't

53

miscarried? They would be twenty-three now. I could even have been a grandma myself. In the dark fog of my room that lost baby hangs over me. The wisp of an almost child gathering like a noose around my neck. To mis-carry suggests I did something wrong. Was that my fault too?

A whistling noise in the house sounds like Dave's laboured breathing. Something I don't miss. His jagged breaths used to claw at my ears as I read or tried to sleep, even with Dave beside me, sleep didn't come easily. Do his deep breaths keep someone else awake now? He lives a mile onto the mainland yet it may as well be a million miles for the times he bothers to visit Jake.

The whistle noise sounds again. Maybe the wind travelling through the chimney? Or down the side of the house. Possibly the tumble dryer. Did I leave it on? Or was it Jake whimpering in his sleep? Or Matthew visiting?

'Jake?'

He doesn't answer. If I get up now, the chill will penetrate my feet and the bed will lose its warmth. Should I check? I think so, especially after tonight's revelations. As I reach his door, avoiding the *Titanic* floorboard, his breath hisses as it passes the gap in his front teeth. He's breathing. I tiptoe back to my room and rescue what is left of the warmth in my bed.

My empty bed.

Should I call Dave? I feel no obligation to let him know about

Jake's illness. Or whatever it is. Google says it's not serious. He chose to be absent. Once at antenatal group, Jayne, the one who looked the most mumsy, talked about her love for her husband and her two children. The second child had given her superior parenting prowess. Been there. Done that. Got the t-shirt. All of us eyed her with equal amounts of suspicion and awe. She made her husband do date nights. Once they watched a tsunami movie and talked about who they would save if they had to choose. Her husband said her. She was furious he wouldn't save the children first. He had some rationale or other but none of us cared to hear it. We all agreed he was a complete bastard for even considering saving his wife. I would always choose Jake. Even before Dave left.

The whistling stops but now I can hear the tumble dryer spinning. Every so often it churns the contents over, airing them through, shaking out stubborn creases. I didn't turn it off. I star-fish across the mattress and start to imagine the vibration of the tumble dryer reaching me through the ceiling, the floorboards, the divan base. The cotton of the sheet rippling with the gentle turn of the drum. I let it tumble me towards sleep. My hip bones, my pubic bone, act like pressure points as they push down into the mattress. I have fifty-five days left on the bed's guarantee. The hassle of returning a mattress though, who would bother? If you suffer with insomnia can you claim your money back? Would they expect a doctor's certificate to prove you usually sleep soundly and the mattress must be causing the sleeplessness, rather than some underlying condition?

I know the doctor's receptionist will try and fob me off on Monday, guarding the doctors' appointments like a Mandalorian. I hadn't understood that series at all. I roll over and practise the voice I will need to use. Delivering the words in an unequivocal tone. I will mimic my mum's officious telephone voice. I will secure an appointment for Jake. *Come hell or high water,* as my mum would say. Where on the ocean is she now? Hopefully she's found some other single pensioners on board, as she planned. And her snoring hasn't had her thrown overboard. Staring at the world map on the wall I attempt to track my mum's cruise ship with my eyes. Focusing on the expansive blue water.

Tap. Tap. Tap.

The gentle sound of next door's wind chime clacking on the fence panel creeps into my ear like a worm. Earlier I'd seen my metal one discarded on the patio, its melody lost until I bother to get the step ladder out the shed to rehang it. I try to follow the rhythm of the hollow wood, and the turn of the tumble dryer at the same time. I try not to fight the chance to sleep.

35 Days

Cramp uses its vice-like grip to throw me out of the arm chair.
My head fizzes, like I dozed off. I stretch my calf out and sit
back down. I tilt my head left, then right, until my neck clicks.
My nap feels restorative so any fatigue I thought might carry
me up to bed, evaporates. I can smell something musty.
Sniffing, I lean into my armpit and take a deeper breath in
through my nose.

It's not me.

Smudge, curled up on the opposite sofa, looks guilty.

'Is it you, Smudge? Have you left me a present?'

Is it in the gap under the kitchen kick boards (ill-fitting and
without Dave they'll stay that way) or in the space behind my
armchair? I lean over the winged sides. Nothing. I begged Dave
for this chair. He called it old-fashioned but I put my foot down.
A reading chair for my studies. When did I last contact my
course tutor? Am I still on sick leave there too? The buttoned

back reminded me of Sherlock Holmes but it is impossible to slouch in. Sherlock didn't seem like the slouching-type so I suppose it is fit for purpose. Smudge uses it as a scratching post so little cotton loops have broken free of the weave, littering each side. It looks shabby now. I check under the kitchen cupboards but find nothing responsible for the musty smell. I sniff my clothes again.

Definitely not me.

It could be from outside; the North Sea dredging up some ancient rotting seaweed. Salty spume coating the pebbles on the beach. I open the lounge window and lean out. The moon with its cratered surface glowers at me. I'd read something about a super moon on Facebook earlier and how unusual human and animal behaviours are often attributed to it. The moon affects Sheppey more than any place I have ever visited. The tide, guided by the lunar cycle, eats away at the edge of the island, pushing and pulling at its identity. My grandmother warned against Moon-Pall. *The bare moon on your face causes lunacy, love. Don't be going out unless your head's covered.* I lean back inside the house and out of its reach.

Earlier that afternoon, we walked the length of the beach, from Minster to Sheerness, navigating our way between overzealous cyclists (all the gear and no idea — probably Dave's mates) and mums with all-terrain buggies crunching on the stray shingle and sand as it wisped in swirls over the concrete sea wall. Jake raced ahead on his scooter. I called out to him a few times, my voice lost in the wind, but I stopped bothering after a mile. After all, he never left my sight. He appeared to be as worried about losing me as I was about losing him. We gazed out across the rippling waves and I pointed out *SS Richard Montgomery's* three masts like I always do. He would have been disappointed if I hadn't. I read the painted words, creeping up each step of the sea defence, reminding every visitor that despite its friendly seaside town reputation, Sheerness isn't safe. I rushed through the last line '*you can see the end of the world from here*' before Jake could make a glib comment about the coming of World War III.

He never tired of hearing the tale of the US warship sinking into the sediment in 1944 whilst carrying 1400 tonnes of live ammunition. Despite being dormant for decades, the danger was close enough to excite him, whilst removed enough to seem safe. Last week a paddle boarder ignored the warnings and took a selfie of himself touching one of the protruding masts. Did he know the gamble he was taking? Only a mainlander would be so stupid. Not that being a native Swampy guarantees you don't do stupid things. I love to tease Jake that the three masts are perches for sea sprites: magical fairies that watch Swampies and set curses on those who deserve them. Any bad behaviour and he would have to face their wrath. Much more effective than the threat of no presents from Father Christmas.

While in Sheerness, we stocked up on supplies for his Scout trip. Batteries for his torch. A new bowl and mug set with clever interlocking cutlery. I didn't think about the nights he would be away. My first nights alone in the house since Dave left. Jake's empty room. Matthew's room. Jake's Scout troop had organised the midweek trip, gaining special permission from school for them to miss term time. He would never forgive me if I didn't let him go.

We crossed the silty fields on the way home, Jake pulling strands of grass through his fingertips. I somehow ended up overburdened with his scooter and the shopping but his carefree steps stopped me asking for his help. Sheep grazed as we passed through the narrow corridor where the coastline encroaches on the farmland. The fresh air stimulated Jake's appetite until he insisted on fish and chips, with enough vinegar to flood Sheppey's marshland. We raised a chip to Grandma and speculated which Mediterranean island she might be disembarking at next. Jake followed his dinner with an ice-cream — Mr Whippy-style — a treat forever tarnished for me after being warned about the listeria lurking inside the dispensers, waiting for me to succumb to the indulgence and deform my unborn child. I got an extra flake and munched on that instead.

Could dairy be responsible for Jake's condition?

How many people were now dairy intolerant? When I was at school no one was allergic to anything other than peanuts and bees, never mind being intolerant to whole basic food groups. I bet the figure is in the millions now. The staffroom noticeboard at work has rows and rows of pupils with allergies, many life-threatening. If dairy didn't mean cheese, I could give it up, but life without Brie and bacon paninis would be less fun. Jake's dairy consumption surpassed most people's. He survived on cereals with gallons of milk, hot chocolate, milkshakes, cheese strings (if they were on special offer) and eggs galore. Not that eggs are dairy. I could ditch eggs and milk from my diet: unfertilised chicken ova (*periods actually* Jake once laughed, as he corrected me) and cow's breast milk. Bile mounts in my throat. When I expressed milk so Dave could feed Jake, I couldn't even try my own to test its temperature. On principle really. It came out of me, prepared and ready to go, like a gloriously nutritious ready meal and after spending hours using an electric pump that sounded like the Millennium Falcon with the suction power to rival a Dyson, Dave could test the temperature of my reheated fluids himself. Why did trying my own breast milk gross me out when drinking a cow's seemed normal? Something somewhere in society has gone wrong.

Once we were back in Minster, before heading up our road, I stopped Jake on the high path and made him absorb the view. I caught my breath and we held hands as we leaned over the sloping cliffs. They disappeared in front of our feet. The North Sea consumes the island's boundary so you can't see where the land ends. Jake claimed he could see France but I knew it was wishful thinking. I changed the subject. I didn't want to talk about his school trip. The salty air brushed my lips, making me thirsty. Jake dropped my hand as a group of boys, not friends but pupils from his year, passed us on the path. Once we were alone again, his soft fingers re-entwined with mine and he started to ask about his appointment. I had rang the out-of-hours number on Saturday morning, putting on my forceful voice and surprising myself when I managed to book an appointment for Thursday.

Will they know what it is? Will they have to look at my bum?

I don't know. Maybe. We will just have to wait and see what they say, Jake. I could see him counting down the hours until his diagnosis. I didn't have the heart to tell him that the only thing that would happen on Thursday would be a promise of a referral. Best case scenario.

My eyes return to the looming moon and I close the window. The humid air outside smells sweet so the musty aroma has not come from there. The floral hit must be the relaxing scent of the climbing jasmine that covers the boundary fence between Malcolm's garden and ours. Blossom litters my driveway like little white stars forming constellations along its length. Dave moaned about the collection of garden debris accumulating in our drive so often that I now relish the scent and the scattered petals. Maybe if I open the window upstairs, it will act like a herbal sedative, a brew of salt water and pollen to help me drift off.

I check my wrist. Still the right side of midnight.

Once upstairs, I open the bedroom window until I reach the limit of my arm. Keeping my head inside and away from the full moon, I use my fingertips to push it an inch further. The musty smell has been whisked away by the sea breeze but I leave the blind open in case it comes back. Sitting on the end of the bed, the cloud starts to cover the moon. Its edge the colour of steel. I try not to pose any cosmic questions to the universe even though they drift through my mind.

If the cloud reveals the moon before 23:56 Jake will be fine.

If the moon remains under the cloud's arrest then the prophecy will come true.

Deals with the devil, my mum called them. She always threatened, *no good will come of it*. Years ago, I visited a fortune-teller. She disapproved of that too and often reminded me how silly spiritualists were.

The fortune teller had been recommended. I went with a group of girlfriends and queued outside the farmhouse for our readings. Waiting at the threshold of the white clapperboard property, complete with rotting window frames and red roof tiles made of rich clay. I could feel the possibility of the

unknown in my bones. There had been no mention in my
reading of me losing a child.

23:59

The clouds pause in front of the moon. I back away from the
window.

The fortune-teller had seemed old and ridiculous, as
decrepit as her house. The scallops of her net curtains wafted in
and out of the open window as she held my hands together in
hers. An ouroboros tattoo, a faded circle of a serpent, twisted
around her wrist. The blue of her veins rippled across the
creature's skin.

At twenty-seven, my irrational fear of dying young must
have been etched on my face. Her first words were ones of
reassurance. *Don't worry I'm not going to tell you anything
awful.* I believed that promise only existed to protect people.
Not that the mediums didn't know awful things. No one wants
to hear that a tragedy will befall them, especially if they're
paying for the privilege. Bad for business.

The woman knew about my miscarriage, claimed the
unborn child had been a girl. My new car (now dying in a scrap
yard somewhere, I still miss it) and my contact lenses also came
up (although that wasn't a huge leap from the glasses I was
wearing). *Lucky guesses,* Dave said when I once told him about

the visit. But the words of reassurance and comfort that came via my uncle's spirit, a cosmic hug was the term the clairvoyant used, filled me with a boundless joy that seeped out of my pores all afternoon. That was real. If I visited again, and begged her for her premonitions, even bad news, would she give them to me? Would my dad come through this time?

A car door slams.

I lean towards the window again and catch Hugh from across the road getting out of his car. Their newly renovated bungalow opposite — all Scandi-cladding and grey metal window frames — makes our house look neglected. But as Dave said, *it's still a seventies dormer bungalow underneath all the polish*. Hugh crunches across his gravel driveway. A deep layer of stones, the most recent addition to their landscaping, had made next door's wild plot, with its border of brambles poking through the broken fence, look even more unsightly. The delivery lorry had blocked our un-adopted road for over an hour as the air filled with the splintering noise of stones cracking against each other and the sweeping swoosh of gravel being raked into place. Their security light beams onto Leanne, who wobbles over the stones, tottering after her husband. Her stilettos flashing their red soles, even from this distance. Leanne works for some ad agency in Soho and likes to shop in Selfridges. We have nothing in common.

Hugh. Please. I'm sorry.

Blip. Blip. His BMW locks clunk with a sound exclusive to German engineering. He disappears into their Italian tiled hallway before Leanne even makes it to the symmetrical topiaries guarding their front door. No marital bliss there either. Maybe the sea sprites do send curses across the North Sea, and into Swampies' bedrooms. I don't like being called a Swampy, nor an Islander. Derogatory words that remind me of my old English teacher ranting about otherness in *The Tempest*. Caliban would have been a Swampy.

Leanne's demanding squeals leak out of their newly insulated walls and across the street. The tide must be in, the air feels heavy with it and the lack of tidal rhythms makes the street quieter than usual. I shiver with the breeze. A sliver of moon remains visible behind the thick clouds, and I can sense rain waiting to fall. I know autumn must follow summer but every year I wish it wouldn't.

Closing the window, I slip into my pyjamas and stroke the sheep grazing across my stomach. Lie down, empty your mind and sleep.

I check my alarm is set. *Try to develop a morning routine to encourage a healthy sleep pattern especially if you are not working.* No matter how sensible Phil's advice sounds, his condescending tone makes it difficult for me to want to comply. But I do desperately want to sleep, so I try. I skip cleansing my face and go straight to moisturiser. A sort of compromise. Some semblance of a routine, if not all of it. Moisturising remains the priority as everything seems to be drying up since I turned fifty. My skin itches with it. Scratching at work is embarrassing but at home, on sick leave, there is nothing to stop me itching until the redness of blood threatens to break through. I lean into the pillow and begin to use my nails across my skin, the pleasure of scratching the itch comforting.

34 Days

I stare at the large fold-out puzzle board covering the middle of my bedroom floor. Earlier, bored and desperate for a distraction, I resorted to Jake's unfinished birthday present: a black and white blueprint of Thunderbird 3. Anything to stop me thinking about the Scout trip. I now have one piece left and one gap. They don't match.

A stabbing pain attacks the point of my spine where it reaches my neck, reminding me to take a break from the jigsaw. We completed the edge weeks ago but it lay untouched until today's drizzle pushed me back to it. Jake might be annoyed if I finish without him. Its monochrome design basks in the orange glow of the bedside lamp, gloating at beating me. Taunting me. The ill-fitting piece a misfit. Like me.

Could the wrong piece have ended up in the wrong box? No. I tore the plastic seal open with my own teeth. And of course jigsaws begin whole until some sociopathic machine carves them up into miniscule pieces so someone with excessive leisure time (or a sleeping disorder) can reconstruct them. Although it will never look as pristine as it does pre-cut, the glory of the completed jigsaw will always satisfy me more. I try the piece again. I lean on my right wrist until the strain threatens to cause a hairline fracture, but at least it alleviates the pain pulsing in my neck. Four sides, four options and not one fits.

Concentration makes my eyesight cloud over. Shadows from the lamp must be hiding the solution. I place the palm of my hand on the glossy image. Moving like a rippling wave, I begin to feel it instead. My naked eyes won't reveal the error but maybe my hands can. I mine sweep the rectangle. A thousand pieces of cardboard locked into place, except one. Left and right. Top to bottom. The shadow from my body, the enemy. I twist the lamp's spring-loaded frame to try and reveal the jigsaw's deformity.

I stand. My spine cracks. Arching backwards, I reach my arms above my head, stretching out until my fingers skim the pendant lightshade. It swings to and fro, interrogating the jigsaw. I move over to the bed and sit down. Looking over it, I notice the bird's eye view helps. Remembering that squinting at artwork can clarify an image, I scrunch my eyes into slits. Sipping my cold tea, I think about the wine I would have preferred to accompany the jigsaw but the doctor said not to mix it with the blue tablets. I keep scanning left to right. 'Got you!' The culprit sits a fraction above the gap, wedged into the wrong space. I pop it free with my nail and place the correct piece in before sliding the final piece into place above it. I stroke the silky surface of the completed image, momentarily satisfied. Returning to the edge of the bed, I keep my eyes on the puzzle; enamoured by the completeness of it. I close my eyes and let myself fall backwards.

Holding still, I try to sink into the mattress, forcing myself down into the buttoned surface. My lower back aches. I sit back up again and fumble in the bedside table to retrieve a make-up wipe to remove today's eyeliner. I pull at the delicate skin around my eye. I know the stain always stubbornly clings to the top of my eyelid even though I didn't apply it there. Unfortunately, fifty-one year old skin is loose and malleable enough to transpose the black kohl pencil into a mirror image above its intended neat line. I fold the wipe over on itself and try again, pressing harder and undoing all the hard work that Lancôme, Mum's idea of a luxurious birthday present, put in.

Who do you wear make-up for? Phil once probed us in our group counselling sessions. Always pushing our buttons.

I wear it to make me feel confident. I tried not to sound defensive. Phil insists on questioning our motivation for everything.

But why do you feel more confident wearing make-up?

Can't I just wear it because I think it looks nice? Who am I kidding? Even with make-up I can't look in the mirror for more than a second or two without grimacing.

I toss the wipe in the wicker bin and think of dolphins choking on my waste. Or the seals we had watched bob amongst the over optimistic surfers in Norfolk. We'd spotted one most days; their silky heads emerging from the murky North Sea like oversized new-born kittens, oily and fresh from the womb. I will invest in washable cotton pads next time. Although I will be removing make-up for six years before my investment will pay off. *Make sure you're saving the planet for me, Mum* — Jake, my eco-warrior. I often watch him retrieve my unwashed yoghurt pots from the waste bin to rinse and recycle. I pretend not to notice.

I squirt moisturiser into a marble-sized ball in my hand. A ball that Mum promised would make my neck look smoother and less like a concertinaed Christmas decoration assembled from recycled crepe paper. Making the recommended upward circular motions, I push at my skin, as if my massage will undo fifty years of physics. My fingers press into the hardness of my skull. Lingering on my cheekbones, I trace each eye socket, moving across my brow and down the ridge of my nose. When did my skin get so thin that I could feel death underneath it? Celebratory Day of the Dead skulls painted with marigolds and monarch butterflies display more signs of life.

71

Tonight sleep bobs in the distance like a ship circling off the coast of Sheppey, beyond the Swale and The Medway, out to sea, forbidden from anchoring in the harbour. Inaccessible like *SS Richard Montgomery*. Since the drizzle stopped, there has been little cloud and I know the stars will be waiting if I can face the night air. The moisture in the sea air will touch me with its damp coldness. How do I have such dehydrated skin when I live on an island surrounded by water?

Even inside the house, my hands and feet are the temperature of meat resting on a butcher's block, so I pull on a pair of Dave's hiking socks (finders keepers) and stretch a sweater over my head as I walk downstairs. A hot drink and the fleece blanket we stash by the back door for star-gazing will keep the chill at bay. I grab both and make my way into the garden.

The moon hovers above the horizon, as if afraid of heights. I fold myself into our wooden garden bench. Covering my shoulders with the blanket, I push my spine into the hard teak to try and unravel the knot niggling me after leaning over the jigsaw. I focus on the moon, straining toward galaxies I cannot see. How insignificant we are in the universe. The damp bench seeps into my pyjamas, so I stand and walk down to the end of the garden. Looking back at the orange light of the kitchen, the propped open door gapes at me. Leaving Jake, and my heating bill open to an attack. I'd left the door open so I would hear him. No one is going to enter while I am at the end of the garden, are they? What's that statistic? Ninety percent of victims know their attackers? Unless Malcolm loses control of his hedge trimmers in a fit of rage or Leanne decides to get violent with her Louboutins, he is probably safe. Jake's safe. Here with me on this island.

He's safe.

He's safe.

He's safe.

As I reach the garden's boundary, my toes catch on an old stepladder leaning against the fence. Jake likes to stand on it, like Captain Jack on his bird's nest. He stares out to sea and counts the gulls catching the thermals before they swoop down on unsuspecting walkers. *Gulls Mum, not seagulls, they are just called gulls. I have told you before. You need to learn that before you teach science.* I climb to the top step and use my elbows to balance on the fence and pull the blanket tighter. The peaks of the waves chase each other in the distance. City-bound people must be claustrophobic without being able to watch the sea disappear in front of them. Their breathing curtailed and their minds hemmed in by bricks and concrete. The glass of the skyscrapers must reflect back infinite amounts of man-made material. Does being amongst all those people make them feel part of something? In a way that someone looking out to the blankness of a limitless ocean cannot? Does the world seem smaller in the city? More comprehensible? The moon's brilliance ripples across the water like an unwound bolt of silk, like the train of my wedding dress. We made it from my mum's gown: unstitching one memory to create another. Something borrowed. Not that it brought me luck. What a waste of a beautiful dress.

All my hems are frayed too. Everything's coming undone.

33 Days

20:52

In the palm of my hand, I gather the crumbs from Jake's almost-toast. *That's not toasted, that's warm bread,* Dave used to tease. I bang and clatter, putting away the jam and spreadable butter, trying to ease my frustration. I must encourage him to start cleaning up after himself. My dad enjoyed jam, layered over at least a centimetre of thick, salty butter. Seedless raspberry. His jar of Finest jam sits in the fridge. I refuse to finish it. Like Jake, he also left his pots on the side, unwashed and ready for the cleaning fairy to stack in the dishwasher. Mum admits she misses his dirty dishes. Strange the moments that make you miss them. I scatter the memories into the bin with the crumbs and think of Jake with jam around his mouth. We had rushed off after school to catch the bus to Scout camp. Jake one step behind me, cramming the double layer of toast and jam into his mouth as we rushed up our pot-holed road to Minster's Working Mens' Club where the minibus would pick them up. I hope he got something more nutritious after pitching their tent for the last camp out of the season. It probably would have been hotdogs. Nutritious food may have to wait until he gets home. He will get home.

The clatter of the bin lid echoes in the empty kitchen. Jake, a quiet, Lego-building child last year, now manages to fill the house with explosive squeals of Xbox-induced delight and horror. During early evenings, he battles with friends, buys new skins and mimics Fortnite dances with considerable aplomb. With his headphones on, I catch his side of each conversation, and remind myself that everything I say is, in all likelihood, being broadcast into at least three of his friends' bedrooms or worse still, front rooms. The kettle growls into the Jake-free silence, expanding with each second. I silence the roar with a flick of the switch and reach for Whittards Sleepy Infusion; it promises 'a herbal lullaby of camomile, lavender, liquorice and linden flowers'. The aroma hits my nostrils and I inhale the flavoured steam deep into my lungs in case the remedy evaporates before it cools enough for me to drink.

Balancing my favourite china cup in one hand and a biscuit in another (with an extra between my teeth), I head to the front room and flick on the TV. The remote control remains where I left it. This is what life will be like without Jake. Organised and predictable. The remote control will wait for me where I left it. The fridge will remain stocked for days on end. My stomach aches for him. In Jake's absence, all I want to do is end the day and start again tomorrow when he will be on his way home. But I know my brain won't let me. Another episode of *Broadchurch*, my cup of tea and a sleepless night and I will be one day closer. Then I'll stroll up to the club and collect him and his dirty clothes (knowing there will be a neatly folded towel and unused flannel at the bottom of his bag). The presence of Detective Inspector Alec Hardy on the TV screen reminds me of the unpredictable nature of life. How it can flip on the roll of a di. All the dangers Jake faces out in the world when I am not with him swim around my head. I trust the Scout leaders to keep him safe (I'd scanned the programme details and the long-haired bohemian is not attending) but as Jake has now progressed from a Cub to a Scout he is allowed to take a pen-knife to camp and it made the potential for an incident bump up the Richter scale a few notches. I shake my catastrophising thoughts away, and blow on my tea now I've finished my biscuits.

I sip the lilac coloured drink. The flavour is surprisingly pleasant despite its floral overtones. Subtle. I look into the front garden and catch a glimpse of my reflection in the window. Ignoring my haggard stare, I try to focus beyond it. The evenings are drawing-in. When I dropped Jake off, the gloaming hour with its purple bruises scarring the clouds, added to my parental neurosis. Jake coughed as the cloying diesel fumes from the volunteer's minibus filled his chest. I made sure the window near his seat was closed. He wore Dave's gift, the Scout-approved Swiss Army knife (bought without my permission and nearly confiscated by me) on his utility belt. I tried to ignore it but his pride meant he showed it to everyone and the metal casing hit his belt buckle with a clang every time he swung his mammoth rucksack over his shoulder, in case I'd forgotten about its potential for danger.

David Tennant's voice reaches out of the TV and promises me, with quiet reassurance, to find whoever is responsible for the murder. The thirty-second counter to the next episode appears on the screen. I tuck my feet under my bum and cover my knees with a blanket. Leaning back into the sofa as the credits roll over the screen, I close my eyes and settle in for the night. Without Jake, I refuse to go upstairs.

01:32

A door slams.

I jerk awake.

The dream absorbing me shoots from my mind, as if it never belonged to me. Its memory nothing more than a whisper in my head. I try to close my eyes to retrieve it. Blackness fills the room.

The blip-blip of Hugh's BMW and the sound of angry tyres

ripping across stones tears through my single-glazed windows. With one salary, when will I ever be able to afford to replace the windows now? I pull the blanket off my legs and place it around my shoulders. I cup my hands around my eyes and lean into the glass to see who stormed out on who this time. Hugh's vehicle reverses off their drive with a spin of gravel spurting from the wheel arches.

I turn and follow it, striding outside and leaving the front door open behind me. Two glowing red eyes light up the rear end of the vehicle which turns left at the junction, towards Leysdown. It must be Hugh driving. His mum owns a chip shop on the seafront and lives above it. Leanne, not a native Swampy, would have headed right, off the island and towards her own mother on the mainland. I detect a hint of snobbery from Leanne every time we speak. As if growing up on Sheppey makes us inferior somehow. Foreign, in an excluded way, rather than the more exclusive kind of foreigner. As I stand on the door step, I can feel my hair absorbing the moisture. Expanding with each drop. How does Leanne manage to live by the sea and maintain frizz-free hair? I remind myself smooth hair does not make Leanne a better person. Only a neater one.

A metal clattering startles me until I realise the spectral sounds travelling across the darkness belong to Malcolm's Jack Russell, his chained collar clanking against the latch of the lead.

'Evening! Or should I say morning? Bloody dog's so old he's

no bladder control. No one should be out at this hour, should they?' I half smile and drop my head; my eyes drawn to my bare feet. I grip the blanket tighter, covering myself. Malcolm doesn't wait for an answer. He takes his dog inside and closes the door.

From the front garden, the percussion of the waves rolls over me. Swishing through my mind. Hypnotising me. I step forward and look back up at Jake's empty room. I turn back around and head towards the cliff path. The soft moonlight guiding my fingers to the wooden rail, leading me down through the eroding cliffs. Years ago, two acres of Sheppey plunged into the sea. I squeeze the handrail a little tighter. Splinters from a damaged section, catch my skin. I reach the steps to Minster's beach and allow the trance-like state I fall into when watching the ocean wash over me.

The base of the sloping cliffs formed from rich alluvial soil are now soft London clay; proof the island was formed in the delta of an ancient river millions of years ago. A place with sub-tropical temperatures and exotic birds. Another Jake science fact. Maybe he'll be a science teacher. If he grows up. He revels in the history of our island, his interest piqued by a local geologist who visited his school and convinced him to join Fossil Hunters, a club over at Warden Point. Soil, gravel and grass begin to morph into coarse shingle beneath my feet. I've reached the beach.

The gentle slapping of the waves on the shore drowns out any road noise, distancing me from my life. A sea breeze whistles through long grass and my body sways with the clumps of marram loosely rooted in the face of the cliff. The water, an inky blend on the horizon, drags me towards it. Sharp stones pinch at the soles of my feet as my toes reach the water. I pause as the icy chill snatches my breath away. Fresh hornwrack in the strandline tickles my feet so I flick it away with a kick. I stand still and breathe in as my feet are submerged. As the tide recedes, the surface dissolves beneath my feet, swirling and reforming underneath me, unsettling my balance. The scent of lemons released from the seaweed sharpens my focus. *Try to live in the moment, Vivian.*

My eyes drift upwards, catching sight of the Milky-Way stretching across the navy blue sky. A swirl of stars advertise another universe far, far away. Does Jake, under the tutelage of a Scout leader, look at the same stars and galaxies? I shake my head. 'No.' He will be in bed now, on his roll-out mattress. No airbeds allowed. Barbarians.

I walk away from the water and lean on the remains of a concrete block, some washed up remnant of the World Wars left in the sea. Oversized litter reclaimed by nature. Weeds cling on, hanging like forgotten dreadlocks. The tide persists, sweeping the sand in and out with the waves. Each time it takes another grain, and another, until it reinvents itself. The island reshapes, day by day, becoming something new but remaining familiar at the same time. If it wasn't for the dredgers, the arm of the sea at the south would silt over and join us to the mainland. Like the isles of Harty and Elmley now swallowed up into Sceapig: Sheep Island. I listen but no bleating reaches me tonight.

The beach is empty. Empty like my house.

A sudden vision of my front door alarms me. Did I leave it unlocked?

I trot to the path to start my ascent. Each lungful of sea air tightening my chest. Going down was easy. Climbing's harder. With my reserves depleted, the gradient works against me. I blame nature's poor design, putting beaches at the bottom of cliffs.

I pull on the fence and take the last step up and onto our unadopted road. Underfunded by the residents, its surface craters and crumbles beneath my feet. Like everything on the island it is bleached by the sun, and blown sideways. Muddy water lingers in potholes and I wonder if whelks and hermit crabs might confuse them with rock pools. 'Focus, Viv.' My words bounce along the edge of the road where the damp grass verges cushion my feet. I hope the island's dog walkers have been conscientious. Why did I come out without shoes? Malcolm's security light stretches across his boundary and as I step on the verge in front of his house, the yellow glow illuminates me. I pick up speed to escape the light and cross into my drive, rising on to my tiptoes to avoid the bite of sharp stones. Not only did I leave the door unlocked, I left it wide open. The fluorescent kitchen light at the end of the hallway shines like a beacon for burglars. The blue light from the TV gives the lounge a menacing glow but at least it means no one has stolen it whilst I paddled in the sea. How did I forget to lock up?

Sitting on the kitchen side, I plunge my feet under the cold tap and wash away the clay. It disappears down the plughole in a swirl of reddish brown. Each grain of dirt returning to the water system. Where will it end up? Back on the beach? On a riverbank? In the distance, a gull caws. 'I remembered Jake, a gull!' My protest echoes in the empty house. One more night and Jake will be home. I dry my feet and make another sleepy tea.

I jiggle the front door handle to double-check I locked it and carry my hot drink upstairs, careful to avoid spillages that could scald my damp legs and toes.

04:24

My heavy eyes stare at the dregs of my cold tea and I swirl the sediment like the Swale stirs the silt. Every time I allow my eyes to close, the weight of sleep evaporates and they spring back like a new tide. My bladder nudges my abdomen. I may as well get up and relieve the building pressure.

I wriggle on the toilet seat to get comfortable but then a hot flush gathers across my chest and travels out to my hands and feet making me rush to finish peeing. I stand and pull off my pyjama bottoms and hang them over the towel rail. I need a little more heat to escape from my bare limbs, so I sit on the edge of the bathtub, the cold surface pleasant on my thighs. The inferno inside me subsides.

I stop by Jake's room on the way across the landing, his missing camp blanket and teddy make his room look forlorn. I shrink with loneliness. As I sit down on the edge of his bed, his soft mattress depresses under my weight. A spring twangs. Maybe he needs a new mattress before I change mine again. I slide down under his covers and hold his spare bear to my chest. The one he keeps on the shelf as it is surplus to requirements. We had bought it as a back-up but he never needed it as he was the sort of child who kept important things in sight at all times. I dip my head into his pillow and inhale. Jake-fume. The ultimate eau-de-toilette. Dave and I joked, if we had been able to bottle the smell of baby Jake we'd have been millionaires. Now the smell of hormones, rather than milk, seep from the cotton, with undertones of Lynx Africa. I embrace the pillow and close my eyes, breathing in time with the waves outside.

I hear Jake's voice.

Can I go to the bathroom, Mum?

A waiter arrives at our table, placing steaming plates of rice and curry in front of us.

Really Jake. Impeccable timing as usual. I glare at Dave. I hate the sarcastic tone he uses with him. I look at the restaurant's signage and can see the toilet is out of our sight line but Jake appears desperate, clutching his groin and bouncing in his seat. Our dinner looks delicious. Heavy spices fill our nostrils. Dave shovels forkfuls of tender beef madras into his mouth, puffing out air to avoid burning his tongue. *Okay, be quick and don't talk to any strangers.* I let him go. Keeping my eyes on him until he disappears around the corner. Dave rolls his eyes.

My knife clatters to the stone floor.

I register the blood-curdling scream that caused my reflexes to react and the knife to drop from my grip. I look up. Jake stands in front of me. One hand on the shoulder of his opposite arm. I pull his other hand toward me and it comes away from his body. One remaining tendon stops it from coming off in my hand. Blood pools on the floor. A dog growls in the distance. Jake's face crumples: white as pure linen and lined with tears. *Sorry, Mum.*

I wake to my own scream.

32 Days

23:50

I step out the bath, wrap myself in a towel and rub away the silky residue of clay clinging to the bottom of the tub. A slew of fresh water trickles between my fingertips. Out at sea, fallen Sheppey buildings hide beneath layers and layers of the same fine silt. In the late 1800s, St James' Church dropped into the ocean — the stones sleep amongst the debris of a sunken cemetery. The nave, the spire, the pews: all rotting in a watery grave. A neighbouring public house followed shortly after. Last orders for eternity.

After an hour-long soak, my nails no longer resemble those of an amateur potter. With clean hands, I line up my beach-combing treasure along the edge of the windowsill. I will apologise for fossil hunting without him when I share my findings. I will leave the organising to Jake. He can categorise them how he sees fit: by geologic periods, by location, by size. Watching him examine our finds under his magnifying glass always reminds me of the Argos kit my dad bought me as a teenager. It broke on the second use but I kept it as I liked the way it looked on my shelf. A reminder that there was more to me than the Smash Hits career quiz suggested. We will talk geology and palaeontology when he gets home from Scout camp.

Jake will come home.

Guilt about fossil hunting without him pricks at my conscience; I try to imagine explaining why I went alone but every version sounds like a betrayal. In reality, his absence pushed me down to the beach in search of something meaningful to do. Something to ground me in the present moment. *Try and live for the now, Vivian.* I will blame Phil, if Jake asks.

The Fossil Hunters, or the retired ones anyway, meet on Monday mornings, at the bottom of Warden Point cliffs. Sharing your finds with fellow fossil hunters makes your treasure coveted and in turn more precious. You feel part of something and there is always someone who knows more than you about what you have found — the community are generous with their knowledge. This time however, I waited until evening, to be sure of being alone. I couldn't face a crowd of friendly people and their small talk with my head already full to overflowing with worry about Jake. And I couldn't face any questions about him either. I had followed Marine Parade, walking alongside the new beach huts with their stripes of candy-coloured wood and made my way beyond the newly equipped outdoor gym on Minster's seafront. The council's attempt to attract new visitors to our coastline. Yet with the tinge of fallen industry in the air, the island fails to compete with the seaside charm of Southwold or the Victorian charms of Margate or Whitstable, no matter how hard it tries. We need to celebrate the natural, rugged beauty of the island instead. Its wildlife and unique marshland. We need to attract a quieter kind of tourist. The darkness began to shadow my feet. I left Minster and headed for Eastend. As my steps started to sink with each stride, I knew my feet had reached the mud flats of Warden Point before my head had caught up. The ground pulled at my wellies. I gripped my toes in my boots and clung on.

By dusk, neither of the enthusiastic hunters from the weekend club, or the retired hunters were about. Using a torch to help navigate my way, I crouched over shallow rock pools and sifted through the silty deposits of the North Sea. Squatting over the shapes and swirls in the sand, which hide million-year-old fossils, I contemplated my insignificance in the history of our planet. Plants and extinct sea creatures tried to tell me tales of a Spanish climate once here on Sheppey.

A cramp forms in my calf. Twisting my muscles around my shin bone. I push out through my toes and pull the bath towel tighter around my breasts. Moving onto my tiptoes, I try to make my calf muscles forget my crouched position on the beach. I had stayed for too long.

Once I returned home, I'd scraped and rinsed my findings. A fetid smell had hit my nostrils, as if I had disturbed something long forgotten. There are rumours that the fossils of elephants and crocodiles have both been discovered on the shores of Sheppey. These items sit at the top of Jake's wish list. The shelves above his cabin bed already display a superb crab's claw, a charcoal grey phosphatic nodule with a veined and dimpled surface and they both sit next to the cast of a lobster's burrow that always brings sniggers from visitors with its long, straight body being topped suggestively with the curve of a helmet. My favourites are the ones that make ready-made paperweights — fish vertebrae finely imprinted on the surface of stones. Jake's favourite find remains the pyrite mould of a gastropod, Fibonacci's sequence evident and existing long before its name had been coined.

The joy at the luck of uncovering a shark tooth today had been quashed by Jake missing it. The item appears right under crocodile and elephant on Jake's bucket list of fossils. We'd been hunting since early spring. Would he be excited I'd found one or disappointed he'd missed it? Probably both. He also missed the marsh harrier's last minute swoop from the cliff, using its v-shaped wings to search for prey. I swear I could feel the wind rippling around me in ribbons as it finished its display. I'll do my best to provide Jake with a vivid description, re-enacting the bird's movements with my hands.

I re-wrap the bath towel around my breasts again, tucking the flap in tighter. Using the corner to dry off the shark tooth a little more, the fetid smell of mildew returns. I pull the other towels off the rails and hold them to my face. I've found the culprit of the musty scent. With Jake absent, I can't even blame him for leaving them to fester on the bathroom floor. I deposit all the towels in the wash basket on my way past.

The shark tooth looks magnificent against Jake's white desk. I tidy his unmade bed, the covers still rumpled from my nap there last night. Grabbing his spare teddy from under the covers, along with his panda Pillow Pet, I take them back to my bed to form a nest with the panda in the centre. I climb in between them all and feel held. Stray feathers poke out my pillowcase. I pull one free and stroke the skin on the inside of my wrist with the goose down, leaning my head against his teddy. Rain drops fall outside. The weather turned earlier and now the arpeggio patters ascend and descend with each change in the wind direction. The island attracts rain in great swathes like a magnet drawn to the iron deposits in the marshland. Tonight cattle all over the island will be clinging to the cotterels: the mini hills on each marsh. I used to have a recurring dream of the island flooding: crowds fleeing for the new crossing, over-spilling onto the old King's Ferry Bridge to head to the mainland, whilst true Swampies held their claim to the wetlands, retreating to the higher ground in Minster. Each time I woke, I was never sure which way to run, or swim.

Jake wouldn't survive a flood in his tent if *SS Richard Montgomery* decided to implode tonight. In the garden we have his boat: Jake's Ark. Could we escape a tsunami in that? It sits out the front under an unsightly tarpaulin, fighting for territory with the weeds. *All Swampy boys want a boat*, claimed Dave as he towed Jake's eleventh birthday present home from Leysdown. A father-and-son project he called it. He promised to fit an outboard motor and restore the wood or replace it, if it was rotten. Jake spent hours over his design for the logo that he would paint on the hull. The drawing, faded and bleached with sunlight, clings to his noticeboard under a bent drawing pin. Dave never found the time.

The rainfall persists, as if trying to break the daily fall record for September. I try to identify the individual drops but the cacophony won't let me separate the sounds. A break comes when a wrung dry cloud passes overhead.

I turn onto my left side. The throb in my right hip reminding me of the long trudge up and down the cliffs to and from Warden Point.

There are footsteps outside.

The sole of a shoe squelching in the surface water pooling

on the path to my door. Tilting my head, I listen to see if the footsteps are approaching or retreating. The rhythm of the footfall synchronises with the rain. I sit up. Definitely approaching.

The wind gurgles as it fights its way through the narrow gap between the house and fence. The footsteps pause. A fox barks. As the wind drops or turns its focus to another corner of Sheppey, the footsteps restart. Adrenaline pumps into my chest. Who is outside? I focus on how wet the steps sound. How regular. A familiar sound after years of drizzly Easter camping holidays at Leysdown. I sit up and draw the blind to look out but lean as far back as I can. Staying out of view. The night swallows my reflection. Drops fall from the blocked guttering. I risk leaning forward and watch them land on the tarpaulin stretched over Jake's boat. My heartbeat slows a little. No intruders, only a broken gutter to fix. But no Dave to ask. No dad. My head sinks with the thought of the repair costs.

Escalating bills, fresh air and dusk fossil hunting make my fatigue intolerable. Powerless against it, I pull open the bedside table drawer and pop two blue capsules in my mouth.

31 Days

00:50

Jake's limbs, spread-eagled over his cabin bed, make him look like he will soon outgrow it. I pick at the peeling stickers covering the wooden bed frame as he sleeps. The grey point of the shark tooth peeks out of his clasped fist, its tip smooth and menacing. Scanning the floor, I refuse to be disgruntled with him and his half-unpacked rucksack propped in the corner of his room, dirty washing and unworn clothes spilling from its mouth. How can I be annoyed? He came home.

Anyway, it wasn't tidy before and the new mess melts into the heap already on the floor. Dark circles and puffy halos of skin around his eyes confirm that little sleeping happened at Scout camp. When we had arrived back at the house, he filled the kitchen with stories of rocket juice (a revolting combination of blackcurrant and orange cordial – the colour of used dishwater) and whittling willow branches with his penknife. He presented a knot of wood vaguely concaved at the wider end.

More of a shovel than a spoon. My jaw tenses with the image, for the second time tonight, of a blade splitting his skin. With pride in his voice, he had pointed out the nick on his knuckle where he slipped, the neat oval of dried blood now a claret-red scab. I inhale, pressing my lips together to keep my anxiety inside. I wait before I force my breath outwards and into the room. I control it. There is no need to dwell on the possibility of that accident now.

Pins and needles start in my elbow but soon reach down my arm towards my fingers. I push myself off the bed frame and back out the room, shaking the tingling feeling from my hand whilst keeping my eyes on Jake.

I pull the door to, leaving a small gap to spy through later and pad across the landing, picking up a pile of laundry from the basket to add to the Scout camp detritus. Once loaded into the machine, I leave the kitchen and head to the TV.

02:12

The spin of the washing machine completing its cycle covers the crackling sounds of the bonfire on the closing scene of the season finale of *Broadchurch*. Golden light from the curling flames fill my lounge. The credits roll and the image of the raging fire vanishes, plunging me into darkness. I can still hear the thwack of each punch Olivia Colman delivered into her screen husband's chest. The reverberations of her screams. An invitation to start viewing season two pops up on the screen. I click next and tuck my feet under my bum to stop a chill creeping into my toes.

03:17

With heavy eyes, I turn the TV off and wonder if I should allow myself to sleep here on the sofa. Autumn rattles at the windows. The coastal wind, whips the tarpaulin wrapped over Jake's boat. What's the point in trying to sleep? I get up and look outside. The wind chime still sits in a knot on the path, silenced.

As I move upstairs, I try bringing the wind into my room with a fan. The stuffiness that filled me with fatigue is starting to make me nauseous. I can't win. The breeze and the fan circulate the air around me, alleviating the night sweats (which have not relinquished their hold on me despite the cooling weather outside) but now outside noises disturb me. The waves breaking, the occasional passing car, the knocking of the cat flap. The blow of the fan, with its constant hum sometimes acts as a buffer to the less predictable noises that usually keep me awake. Not tonight. Tonight the spinning blades blur as they cut the air. I close my eyes and try harder to tune into the white noise.

My daily dose of sleepy tea hasn't helped dull my brain activity this evening. Jake's doctor's appointment tomorrow fuels each cell with enough paranoid delusions to cast off my mum's cruise ship. When my mind fills with the horror of Jake's prophecy, no amount of insomnia remedies help. My head thrums with the endless refrain of 'What will the doctor say?' The words act like a lightning bolt passing from conductor to conductor until the spark ignites the fuel source and explodes. *Don't worry about something until you have got something to worry about*, Mum likes to preach. *It's a waste of energy. How many people say they wish they'd worried more in life? No one said that ever.* The wisdom of the old. It sounds so easy. Don't worry. Yet if everyone wishes they did it less then it must be inevitable. Why fight it?

My worry acts like a sentient being with a mind of its own. It watches Jake's every movement. His reluctance to eat, his sore throat, a mouth ulcer, his dry lips, his achy knee, his stitch. Everything a possible symptom. Is he paler than usual? Than other boys? Are the dark shadows under his eyes a sign of some deeper fatigue — more than a child should have? Where is the energy an eleven-year-old boy should exude? Is it the divorce or is it twenty-first century lethargy? A symptom of the times? Or a more sinister disease eating away at his insides?

At tomorrow's appointment, the doctor will be rushed, already thinking about the next patient or still dwelling on the last one. Will they listen to his words or will they quiz me instead? Will they suspect me of neglect? Will they read the fear on our faces and take us seriously or dismiss us as hypochondriacs? I don't want to go in there with melodramatic pleas but I want to be heard. How many times over the years have I left the surgery and arrived home exasperated? Sticking the kettle on while I rant. *Well, that was a waste of time. A virus. Nothing we can do. You'll feel better soon.* Be patient. Don't be a patient.

I have prepared a list of questions. Prepped Jake to make sure he tells them everything, no matter how embarrassed he feels. What else can I do?

I flick the switch so the fan will blow on me, then off me. The oscillating air acting as another distraction.

It doesn't work.

I scan the walls. William Morris wallpaper lines the hallway — another left over from the previous owners. Through the gap in the door, the willow boughs covering the top half, above the dado rail, reach around the aperture of the bathroom. The low energy bulb in the landing lightshade casts a yellowy glow across the pattern. Each thin, flexible stem sprouting a dozen or so leaves. I try counting the intricate lines. Shadows of darker green imitate the veins, giving the two-dimensional print the impression of a living and moving thing. I soon tire of trying to focus on the veins without my glasses so turn my attention to the large leaves instead. No immediate patterns spring out, three, five, then six leaves per branch. The curled tips reveal the pale undersides and the branches, some an aging brown, intertwine with the vibrant green of fresh shoots. The tendrils begin to move on the wall like serpents. I blink, slowly does it, allowing the moving image to stop, to return to its dead pattern. As I opens my eyes wide, the wall is still again. My breathing slows.

I get up to check on Jake.

Reaching out behind his bed frame, is the patch of mould that Dave cleaned off and repainted last year. It's back. Small black mottles breeding and seeping through the plaster. With my palm on the wall, I can feel the water in it, as if the sea is soaking up through the foundations and into his room. It's spreading further out this time. A wide arc of spores. Filling and infecting his lungs.

Jake faces the wall and the black spores; his bum poking towards me. Each exhalation passing through his open mouth with a wheeze. Leaning onto my tip-toes, I reach over and see the white crust clinging to the edge of his lips. I draw in his scent. I stroke his nose and it twitches like the witch I loved watching on TV as a child. Putting my feet sideways on to the cabin bed ladder, I climb up and squeeze into bed behind him. I wriggle one arm under his pillow, trying to turn his face away from the mould. My body cocooning him. His bare arms are cold to the touch, as if the damp from the walls has seeped into his skeleton too. He groans and resettles. I hold him. Feel the softness of our bodies moulding into each other. I love him so much it hurts.

30 Days

23:56

I scan the synopsis of Season 3, anything to avoid the doctor's words swirling around my head. The screen blurs in front of me. I can't face more crime. Even David Tennant's presence doesn't appeal this evening. With a push of a button the screen implodes like a black hole. Pulling my half-read novel from the shelf under the coffee table, I re-read the blurb to try and refresh my memory of what I've read as the first few lines of the chapter made no sense to me at all. Surely the plot line lingers at the back of my head somewhere — something about an alcoholic detective neglecting his family. I remember why I put it down. It won't be any less depressing reading a crime drama than it will watching one.

Searching my bookshelf for another distraction, I admire the fullness of it. Books stacked vertically, horizontally, all crammed into every available space. No gaps from Dave's missing items here. His absence stands out most in the shed where the large open space for his toolbox attracts cobwebs and fallen leaves from the unruly sycamore, blown in by the wind. My fingers trace the spines searching out a book that will make me sleepy with concentration. Victor Hugo's *Les Misérables* fills the space of three novels on the shelf. I bought it from the charity shop on Sheerness High Street after being enamoured with the musical. I liked the film too but my intense dislike of Anne Hathaway marred the cinematic experience for me. As well as Dave's *another bloody song* comments. I pull it off the shelf and examine the cover. The pristine condition of the cheap classic re-print won't withstand many readings before the thin, already yellowing pages will flutter free from the delaminating glue. 'Half a century ago nothing more resembled any ordinary port cochere than that of No. 62, Petite Rue Piepus.' The crackle in my voice as I read the first line echoes in the empty room. I haven't spoken to anyone since Jake went to bed. I close the novel but not before I spot someone's scrawled dedication inside the front cover. Two pencilled words: For John. Not exactly a moving inscription. I flick to the final page, 1583. It doesn't look like John read any of them. I slide it back on the shelf and go to fetch another cup of tea.

00:59

Stumbling to the bathroom with my eyes half-closed, I try to convince myself I am sleepy. I pull the light cord and the string snaps. 'Shit.' The new LEDs flicker to life despite the broken cord. Rotting string to match my rotting life. The stark lighting makes me blink and tighten my eyelids harder. I tie a knot in the two halves — a temporary repair that will have to do. Dave had fitted the flush ceiling bulbs before he left, but I have no idea how to change them so I hope they never blow. Do LEDs even blow?

I release the tap and the roar of water fills the bathroom and then my head. The force of water splashing onto ceramic blurs out my thoughts. With my eyes half-closed, I am unable to see where to apply my face wash so I give in and open them. *A comprehensive skin care routine can prepare your body and mind for sleep.* Did I read that somewhere or is that more Phil bullshit? The white light bleaches my skin whilst the mirror cruelly reminds me that I am paying the price for spending years not following a decent skin care routine. I look away. The hot water is taking longer than usual so I turn the tap until the valves open to maximum. Circling the polishing cleanser across my cheeks, the smell of lemons and lavender takes me to a past family holiday in France. I ignore the memory — any pleasantness of the time erased by our impending divorce. I continue to circle my fingers, avoiding the delicate eye area as instructed. Even if it does feel like a decade too late to be following these instructions.

The bowl of water releases whispers of steam into the room. A thin veil of mist clouds in front of my face protecting me from my reflection. Placing the soft bamboo cloth that came with the polishing cleanser into the water, I rinse and wring. The silky flannel's texture smooths my face as I maintain the loose circular motions needed to make the cream vanish. Rinse and repeat. I always question whether any evidence exists to prove you need to repeat these rituals or if these instructions are motivated by corporate greed to ensure I consume more of the tube of expensive cream than I need to. I return it to the cupboard under the sink where it joins the other half-used bottles of cleanser, toner, moisturiser, face-masks, hair-masks, pore removers and exfoliating creams collecting dust. Why do I never finish them? Years of evidence that I have been attempting to fix something. Fix everything. I should throw them all away. I close the cupboard. I'll do it later.

Prepared by my rituals, I reach my room and position myself in the middle of my mattress. Laid on my front with my right hand under the pillow, I wriggle into the memory foam and wonder how many days are left on the guarantee now. Maybe forty-nine? The fold of my pyjama hem digs into my thigh. I wriggle again until it shifts to one side. Can I deceive my eyes into sleeping? I tell myself rest is enough. No pressure to sleep, only rest. I turn the pillow to the cooler side. Despite the pitch of the night, streaks of light reach under my eyelids. They flick open. Still dark. I close my eyes again and let my vision scan the inside of my eyelids.

I hear a scream.

A curdled cry from a petrified child.

I bolt upright and grab a handful of quilt in my fist. My knuckles whiten as I strain to hear the edge of the scream. It falters, leaving a short hiss behind. I recognise it. The radiator gearing up as the metal contracts. Air pushing and straining and screaming. It fights its way out as my heart rate speeds.

I breathe in to ease my pounding chest. My lungs ache as I stretch their capacity. After I test the limits of my respiratory system, I lie back down, pulling the duvet over my chest. Holding my breath, I ignore the hiss of the radiator, the clinks, and whirrs of moving air. I release my diaphragm and follow it with another deep inhalation to placate my burning lungs. I roll onto my front and bury my face in the mattress. I allow the doctor's words in for the first time since we left the surgery. No need to hold the muscles in my face in place. No need to shield my eyes and my feelings from Jake.

There's nothing obvious. No perianal damage. No distended stomach. But, I am going to put in a request for a blood test. Just to be certain. Bleeding in this way is highly unusual in children. And you'll need to keep a diary of food intake and your bowel movements too. The doctor had directed the last statement to Jake who was too terrified to even blink a response. When we left the surgery, I looked at him and smiled. *See, nothing to worry about.* But I could see him repeating the doctor's words in his head, reading the worst-case scenario into them. *She said, highly unusual though, that can't be good, can it, Mum?* I kept my eyes on the horizon. *Let's focus on the positives until we know any different, yeah?* We had not been fobbed off with a nurse practitioner though. My anxiety seeped out of me like noxious gas: invisible and poisonous. I turned my face away from Jake every time I exhaled.

Will the blood test hurt?

No, I promise it is nothing more than a prick, and I will be there.

But Dad always faints when he gives blood.

You're not your dad, Jake.

Thank God.

Smudge jumps up onto my bed, pushing his small head into my hand. I pull back and tickle him under his chin, using the firm stroke I know he likes, progressing from his ears to the tip of his tail. He pads each paw in a repeated motion, circling on the spot until he decides the exact place in which to settle. I rest my hand on his back and feel it rise and fall with shallow breaths. I try to copy the rhythm so I can go with him to the place he finds peace.

29 Days

23:49

With a final swipe of the dishcloth, the kitchen side looks tidy enough. I force the Calpol bottle back into its allotted space in the old Jacob's cracker tin, its rusty edges and bent lid adding to the challenge. Hoarding our expired medicines and plasters (even those no longer sticky enough to work) is a habit I inherited from my mum. *Waste not, want not.* I must start to encourage Jake to take the cheaper paracetamol tablets next time he needs pain relief. I'll buy the plastic capsules rather than the chalky ones to help. I rinse the sticky strawberry residue from my fingers and wipe them on a tea towel. The attendance officer at school suggested a dose of Calpol and a brisk walk to school might have cleared up his headache this morning and made him fit for class. Friendly advice or a veiled threat? Do kids ever manage to bunk off school anymore? Unlikely with the Stasi-style officers policing all their absences. It was barely past ten when she called. The smell of old dishes remains on my hands. I wash them again.

Why should I have to justify his absence to anyone? Jake had
a good reason to stay home. He needed to recover from the
Scout trip. He looked depleted. Headaches can be symptomatic
of so many things. They shouldn't be dismissed too readily,
especially in children. Imagine ignoring what a child says and
then finding out later that you are too late to do anything about
it. At home I can make sure he is okay, at regular intervals. Not
like at school where they'll make him wait for a break or
lunchtime to go to the office with any complaints. I know the
drill. They'll say, *see how you go*, and by then it could be too
late. They shouldn't want ill children in school anyway and as I
work there you would think they could have a little more faith
in my judgement.

Jake had seemed reluctant to stay home too. He tried to take
back his pain and claim it had passed but he changed his mind
soon enough – once I reminded him of the lack of privacy in
the toilets at school and of his current problem. When I was
younger, a day off sick had been a gift, so rare they were. Filled
with daytime TV and whatever I fancied to eat. No boring
floppy cheese sandwich, Frazzles, Penguin bar and satsuma
(with pips). I made sure Jake had a good day. Even made him
pancakes and let him have a fizzy drink on a weekday. It's not
his fault he's ill.

I kept the house in permanent darkness in case his eyes

were sensitive to the light. You can't be too careful with headaches. Together we watched an episode or two of *Stranger Things* in a cinema-style cocoon, not letting the 15 age rating bother me this time.

Time feels different now.

What if he never reaches fifteen so he can watch it legally? Not that it is illegal. It's guidance, surely? It cheered him up, eased the blow of missing both science and design technology at school. They were studying oceanography. *Mum, did you know that the earth's deepest trench is deeper than Mount Everest is tall?*

By lunchtime, he claimed his headache had passed and had asked to go in for the afternoon session. *You need to rest.* I reassured him. *To recover properly.* Soon his limbs extended across every cushion as he melted into the sofa. I'd done the right thing.

It even meant I got some sleep, dozing in the knowledge that Jake would be in my care all day. No risk of abduction, hit and run, food poisoning or bangs to the head on the adventure playground. In Jake's first year at school, he had slipped from a wet wooden post and smacked his face on the adjacent one. The full weight of his body pushing his delicate features towards the back of his skull. Both his eyes and nose swelled into each other, obscuring his vision and resulting in a hematoma so large and so infected that when they operated to drain it they discovered all the cartilage in his nose had dissolved; disintegrated into a mush of pus that drained out with the liquefied bruise. He had squished his malleable nose this afternoon as the wall in *Stranger Things* pulsed and oozed on the screen.

At home there was no chance of him suffering an allergic reaction to any of the chemicals in science or being accidentally injured by their science teacher, Mr Preston, who had a penchant for dramatic chemical reactions and often mixed chemicals to show off in front of his pupils. Jake had been enthralled since his first week in year seven. The 'theatre of science', his teacher called it. He showed off in the staffroom too. I'm not sure I would have the confidence to be so experimental as a teacher but with my degree on pause, the thought of teaching stretches into the realms of never anyway. And then there's the proximity of the *SS Richard Montgomery* to school. If an off course ship catches that...I shut shake my head to stop it going there. The armed patrols that ominously circled the ship during the 2012 Summer Olympics in case a terrorist took advantage of the island's readymade weapon, still replay in my head.

My mum calls it a ticking bomb. With seven decades of still waters and years of silt, not even the deepest sea trench could reassure her. Jake's school suddenly feels too close to the buried ship. Things nightmares are made of.

I had switched off the TV in the late afternoon to prevent any chance of the horrors lurking in *Stranger Things* making their way into Jake's dreams, turning them into nightmares. He claimed he wasn't sleepy at bedtime but I can't hear him moving around now, so he must have settled. Nightmares would mean sleep...maybe I should watch another episode without him.

00:12

I stand at my bedroom window watching Malcolm next door. The one neighbour on the street whose lights are still on. He is always up late, letting his dog out for a last wee before bedtime. The Jack Russell trots straight across the road and lifts his leg against Hugh and Leanne's new hedges: small shrubs that will one day shut out the rest of the street. Unless the dog's piss stunts their growth first. Malcolm hisses at the dog to come back in. He trots further away and continues to trickle his territory-marking further along the street. Malcolm steps out. He wears striped pyjamas and a plain white tee, more modern than the flannel pyjamas you'd expect for a man his age. He scratches his beard and stops hissing for the dog for long enough to stare at our house. The lights are off but I am conscious of our open windows, both mine and Jake's. I step back. The way he inspects every window is intrusive, especially considering the time. At least the rest of the blinds are closed. They have been all day. Apart from my room, I'd opened them to inspect the street.

I stay still. If I move closer to improve my view, Malcolm will see me and know that I know that he is watching me.

'Psst. Tipper. Inside now.' Malcolm keeps staring, focussing on Jake's room. He shakes his head and pats the dog's bum with his foot, ushering it towards the house with his tartan slippers. He heads back inside but not without a final glance at the whole house. Through the quiet night, the clunk of him locking his front door travels up to my room.

I close the blind and before I climb into bed, I grab Jake's teddy from my floor. It still holds his sweet, stale smell. He hadn't wanted to take it to bed tonight. Its lingering mustiness wrinkles my nose but the heady combination of Jake's saliva, his sweat and any remnants of food he hasn't bothered to wash from his face and hands over the last few years soothe me. I haven't washed it in a long time. I pull it to my nostrils and inhale my son. I close my eyes and think of young Jake.

Four years old. His hair still white-blond and none of his baby curls cut. He fits in my arms and folds himself into my lap. His fingers rub the silky smooth label of his teddy while his eyelids and bottom lip are heavy with sleep. I long for my own fatigue to overcome me. The label on his teddy dangles, hanging by a thread.

28 Days

05:30

Under my legs the wall scratches at my thighs, the last hour of
waiting imprinted on my skin. The concrete trellis wall holds
fast, despite decades of sea fret and coastal winds. Hugh and
Leanne's renovations highlight the anachronistic style of our
wall but Dave always said it wasn't broken so there was no
point in fixing it. We couldn't afford to anyway. I reposition
myself and wriggle around on my navy coat, my pyjama
bottoms flapping in the light wind as I wait for the sun to rise.
Hugh's hurried exit in his SUV a few nights before remains
evident in the furrowed gravel on their drive, a result of his
spinning wheels. The air smells of the rain gathered in the
deeper gullies.

In the distance, street lights bounce off Sheppey's over-
developed housing stock. Every rooftop stretching into the
clouds with their loft conversions and double storey extensions
and towering dormer windows protruding between terracotta

tiles. Tilted skylights and elaborate geometric domed glass roofs that forge their way into the sky. If not the attic space being appropriated, it's garage conversions and conservatories. With space limited on the island everyone maximises their plot. In contrast, vast expanses of land remain swampy marsh, habitable by wild fowl and hooved beasts alone. I return my eyes to my modest home, surrounded by its parched grass, now waterlogged with late summer rain. The abandoned boat and weed-infested borders look wanting compared to Hugh's renovation opposite. I close my eyes and shut out the inadequacies of our house.

When I open them, the window of Jake's room is ajar. I no longer allow him to have it fully open: too risky with Malcolm prowling around so I've limited it to the crack. It's another hour until sunrise and the street is dark. No one is prepared to fund the cost of street lamps on our unadopted road. The only light comes from Malcolm's driveway. I recognise the faint rumble of his boiling kettle. His dog must have him up early again.

What am I doing outside at half five? I don't have a geriatric dog to tend to. I stand up. My pyjamas catch on the concrete edges so I pull the fabric free. My legs wobble. Have I been sat there that long? I start to walk out my stiff limbs, shaking them into the dim light.

Before I realise it, I'm upon the Abbey ruins. My favourite place to watch the sunrise on the island. Not quite the peak of the isle, that's The Mount, but walking distance from my house. My ill-fitting slippers drag along the track, playing a lazy rhythm, as they slap the path. By the time I reach the gatehouse, my toes ache with gripping the hard rubber sole. Not the best choice of footwear for an early morning walk. I drag my fingers along the ancient stone wall and the heady scent of weeds aggravates my nostrils. Pinching the bridge of my nose, I breathe through my mouth instead. I search the ground through the gloaming light for the culprit of the irritant. It must be pollen of a deep ochre, thick on the stamen, to release such a pungent odour. A yellow smell. Nothing but daisies and dandelions nestle amongst patches of marram grass that look as dry as my lawn.

We loved spending Halloweens trailing storytellers through these ruins. Their deep voices weaving tales of persecuted nuns living at the Abbey, dealing with the skulduggery of smugglers. Jake never tired of the same stories. I hope he won't think he is too old this Halloween. A maze of underground tunnels facilitated midnight escapes for the nuns. I look for Lady Grey, who appears to Swampies in her long pale petticoat. Islanders claim you can hear the layers of her cotton skirts brushing the dusty ground. A small bird whistles to its mate as the sun peeks up from behind the gatehouse. It surprises me and I look around for the source.

Where am I? Am I at the Abbey?

'Jake? Jake?'

The ancient ruins absorb the sound of my voice. My eyes dart side to side.

'Jake, where are you?' Nothing.

I am alone amongst weeds and stone walls.

'Jake?'

The wind whistles back. My clothes flutter. I tighten the belt of my coat. Pushing my fingertips into my eye sockets, I manipulate my eyeballs as I grapple with my memory. Something feels off. I look at the sun rising over the coastline. I check my watch and the cuff of my pyjama arm peeks out of my sleeve. A vague realisation hits me. Jake didn't come with me. Jake is at Scout camp. I stretch out my long strides to maximise my pace. I need to get home.

06:59

Malcolm's fetching in his milk as I reach the house. He scuttles back inside without a morning greeting but he takes the time to glance from me to Jake's window and back again. He maybe shook his head but I can't be sure. Embarrassed by my dusty toes and my pyjamas poking out the bottom of my coat, I avoid his gaze.

Does he think I'm crazy?

Surely, he's crazy for ordering milk by doorstep delivery. For staring at the dark bedroom windows of small boys. Doesn't everyone buy milk at the supermarket now?

By the time I reach the top of the stairs, Jake appears out of his room. He's not at Scout camp. Shit. What day is it? Jake's rubbing his eyes and staggering to the bathroom. Hiding behind his morning blindness, he reminds me of a mole breaking the surface for the first time. I smile at him, respecting his anti-social morning mood with good grace. I left him at home. How did I do that? He closes the door behind him and the metallic lock clunks. I ignore my dusty feet and clamber under my covers. Hoping he will join me for a cuddle when he's finished.

27 Days

23:55

I try to focus on the joy of being in bed: the pillow cushioning my neck, the smooth cotton of the sheet on my chilly thighs. I know I should ignore the fact I'm wide-awake. Synaptic connections bounce between my brain cells as if I'm high on drugs. Phil uses science terms like 'synaptic' to try to explain away our symptoms during sessions, as if a medical explanation will prevent it happening again. I rub my legs around the mattress to generate some warmth. Bits of grit from yesterday's early morning walk still cling to the sheets from when I clambered back under the covers in an attempt to disguise my early morning absence from Jake. I sweep my feet until each grain tumbles over the side of the mattress. I pull myself up a little and lean against the headboard when something sharp pricks my skin. A white feather curls out of the pillowcase. I pull it free and trace it across my palm, following my life-line. I imagine Jake's smooth hand, warm and soft in mine as we had walked the beach earlier in the afternoon. His blood test tomorrow won't reveal anything. I know it won't. It won't be that easy.

A shadow reaches into my room from outside and lays claim to the wall. It looks like a face. Lady Grey's ghostly image: blurred elongated features, pale-skinned and in the shape of a full Victorian dress. I blink slowly trying to catch it out. The face is still there. Dark sockets for eyes and blushed grey shadows for cheeks. It could be a young boy. Matthew? I close my eyes. When they reopen, the shadow has passed. I rest my head on the soft velvet, trying to trick my body into sleep. If I stay upright, maybe my body will forget to fight.

Deep nasal breaths tickle my nostrils, as I push the air out the way it came in. My skin feels heavy, my tongue thick. I press it against the roof of my mouth, trying not to swallow, not to move even a millimetre. I can feel my teeth rooted in my jaw. A vein pulsing in my neck. The bubble of water trapped in my ear canal after my bath earlier, threatens to pop. The smell of lavender oil evaporates from my skin. Flotsam and jetsam dart under my eyelids as the light from the hall bleeds through. My irises blossom, like a light installation in my head. Cars travel past on Minster Road, taking advantage of the light traffic, speeding towards Sheerness or Leysdown. Two seaside towns. Two ends of the island. I have folded my arms under my breasts, and they rest on my stomach. The bit of flab I can never shift, no matter how hard I try, squished between the two. My hands clamp each elbow. Holding myself still. Still enough for sleep. A twinge in my calf makes me twitch but I stiffen in an attempt to ignore it. I hold my frame, attempting to ward off the cramp I know wants to twist my calf muscle inside out. I brace myself, my teeth pushing down on each other, harder and harder. I will not move. The cramp keeps travelling up the muscle, bit by bit, until it takes hold.

I fling off the covers and push my toes into the carpet. The pile is no longer fluffy, but flattened and tired from overuse. It's in dire need of replacing. I can feel the melted synthetic fibres where I left the straighteners on, crusty under my toes. The carpet had been newly fitted, when I'd burnt it. Dave had seethed at me for days. *Don't push down, lift your toes up and away.* Dave's instruction comes back to me, frustrating me with his superior knowledge even in his absence. I follow his instruction and the spasm gives. I let my breath go and sit back down on the edge of the bed.

If I am up, I might as well pee.

In the bathroom, I recoil as I spot Jake's latest beach find — his newest prize possession — sitting on top of the cistern as it dries off. After the doctor's appointment on Thursday, we'd walked to Sheerness. There had been no point in returning to school for one lesson. As we strolled along the beach, he had noticed its yellow tail poking out of the shingle. I cringe as I remember my squeal for him to put it down, frightened he would be stung. I nearly bashed it straight out of his hand but Jake pulled away. *Mum, it's just an exo-skeleton. Stop panicking.* He waited for my arms to drop back down by my sides before he trusted me enough for him to hold out the palm of his hand to let me examine his discovery. The chocolate brown shell with eight legs in a lighter shade and the yellow tail curled outwards, still intact. It couldn't have been more than two inches in length but it almost filled Jake's hand. *It must have been washed up from the dockyard. Did you know that there are over ten thousand in the crevices and the railway sleepers in the docks?* I shudder again at the thought of so many scorpions so close to home.

No, I didn't, and I wish I still didn't.

They think they first came over on a ship from Italy.

Oh right.

They are the most northerly scorpion colony and even cooler than that, their shells glow under fluorescent light.

Very cool. I had tried to sound enthusiastic.

The exo-skeleton is too close for comfort, so I shift forward on the toilet seat. After rinsing my hands, I turn off the light and watch the yellow tail shimmer. I pull the door closed until it clicks and I return to my bed.

Night sounds gather around me. I isolate each one until I can hear the one I want, the waves caressing the beach. The wind picked up again today and its deep, angry howls still come and go, the arpeggio of the sea reaching over it to reveal the power of the tide. It washes away the marks of the day, lugworms' spirals dissolve and new secrets are revealed with every sweep of the tide.

Switching on the lamp, I open my new novel. Another attempt at a distraction, *Elizabeth is Missing*. The narrator's mind comes and goes like the North Sea. Her thoughts froth and foam, marbled patterns that make sense and then dissipate until nothing is left to make sense of. At least my own mother isn't disappearing in front of me, gradually losing one brain cell at a time. That would be difficult to witness. Painful. According to her last message, she is living her best life. I turn the page and let the story keep me from sleep.

26 Days

22:21

The car lights trail across my bedroom ceiling reminding me of the glint of the needle in the nurse's hand this morning, her search for his veins, his crumpled face as it punctured the surface of his body. My skin ripples with the memory, as if a living creature writhes inside me. My shuddering body sends the memory on its way and I rub my arms to dispel the rising goose-bumps.

Jake's small hand had clutched mine with a fierce grip making my middle ring pinch the fleshy part of my fingers. It hurt. I'd purchased the ring because its stone symbolised hope and at the time I had needed the reassurance of that symbol every time I looked down at my hand. I was pregnant with Jake and with those blood test results everything teetered on the edge of disaster. As I twisted the ring around my finger it reminded me that there was a chance everything would be okay.

This morning, Jake looked at me instead of the nurse. His closed-lip smile and sucked-in cheeks revealed his silent worries and they streamed into my consciousness where they settled alongside mine. No matter how hard he tried to swallow back his fear, I felt it with him. The nurse's small talk about football didn't help. I'd tried to redirect it to cricket or Lego, something that might catch his attention, but once his eyes caught sight of the needle, nothing could distract him.

I push the thought of the test results away.

Manage what you worry about. Phil always makes it sound so easy.

I bring my knees up and push myself into the headboard. My legs pulse with pent-up energy. I rub the soles of my feet over the sheet and massage my temples with my fingertips, kneading away the stress.

Trying to sleep tonight seems pointless. I reach for the pills in my bedside table and slip two capsules into my mouth.

25 Days

23:03

Weather been terrific. Made some friends and we are heading for Italy next. All is well with me. I hope you are getting some sleep, darling. Tell Jake the food is as amazing as I had hoped. Sending love. Mum xxx

I switch off my phone. *Screens in the bedroom stimulate the brain.*

Jake will be pleased to hear his grandma is enjoying the food. This morning he convinced me to buy him a triple chocolate muffin and a hot chocolate on the way to school. *It'll take my mind off waiting for my results.* A manipulative smile curled at the edge of his lips when he knew he'd won.

So much sugar and all before nine am. When did I let my rules become so breakable?

At least school didn't need to phone me today. I got him there. Parenting win. The surgery said they would call with the results. They hadn't, and I still haven't called Dave.

This morning the sea mist settled on Minster like a soft blanket but by the time I'd walked back from the school run, the warmth seeping out of the soil had begun to evaporate the moisture in the air. The remaining mist had clung to the horizon, blurring the edge where the sea met the sky, eventually though the sun burnt off the rest. Now the gloaming hour has brought the ghost of the mist back. Out the window fog twists down our lane, heading out towards the sea. It licks at the wildness; drawing the green corridor of hedgerows closer together. A tangled web of brambles laced with spiders' silk decorates the borders to the road, each delicate strand clinging onto droplets of sea fret.

The churning whirr of the wind turbines lining Herne Bay and Thanet carry across the Medway like an industry sighing with the effort of adapting. The rhythm of Sheppey's dying industry replaced by clean power. Momentarily, I am glad my father isn't alive to see the island now. Its industrial collapse mimicking the eroding shoreline. Will Jake be able to make a living on the island when he leaves school? The thought of adult Jake is too far into the future to imagine. Unreachable. The wind turbine blades slice the empty air; alchemy turning it into energy. Could Jake take his prophecy and magic a different future for himself? A future full of hope. Would he go to Dave on the mainland? The ocean has kept me on Sheppey but with Jake's prophecy it closes in on us like a threat surrounding its prey. I should have left when I was younger, freer. Yet the time never seemed right. My mum cruises the world, maybe I should lift my anchor a little. Maybe Jake and I should move.

I pull the journal out from under my pillow. I ignore the folded corner. If I look at it, the entry will crawl off the page, follow the spine and entangle itself into my mind. I turn to a blank page instead.

In today's therapy session, Phil asked the group to write a postcard to their former selves. Pre-breakdown selves. *What would you tell yourself now?* In other words, what have you learnt since you've been here?

Do not read old journals from stressful holidays and periods of your life when you struggled with your mental health.

Phil read over my shoulder. *That removes the problem. That's not a solution. You need to work out what you are going to do – you can't build a time machine and erase an event. What we want to know, Vivian —* the shape of my name on his lips rang with disappointment *— is how you would cope differently now. Don't you feel like a different person?*

I am not sure I do, but I kept that to myself.

23:42

My pen hovers over the page. Phil asked me to start writing again. *Constructively.* I should have bought a new journal but there are pages left in this one, as if I abandoned it mid-year.

I haven't written at all since I discovered the old entry, afraid to give my concerns space on the page. Space for them to grow, to stretch, and strengthen. In case they take over.

He told me to write about each day. To keep it neutral. I scribble down the insignificant words about the walk to and from therapy, my steps along Sheerness High Street, how I stood outside the sweet shop, reading the signs in the window. Faded black Sharpie advertising reduced prices, a pale violet scrawl remained — bleached by the sun. A small child spitting sweet after sweet beyond the edge of his pushchair. The way he leant over the side as he sucked each fish-shaped jelly in and then, after a hearty nasal inhalation, he propelled it out of his mouth and onto the path. Each time the projection became more powerful and his aim more accurate. The fish writhed in front of me, damp with saliva. Wet fish floundering on the street. A rainbow of rejections.

The pensioner everyone called Old Joe cycled past as I lingered on the kerb — my indecision stopping me mid-step. Should I cross the road to the meeting room or should I walk over the sea wall, down onto the beach and towards the sea? I could keep walking until water splashed over my feet, then my ankles, followed by my knees as they disappear into the heavy salt water. By the time I reach my waist, the cold will take my breath away. Gasping, as the water reaches my breasts next. My nipples will harden. The pain will be exquisite. My progress through the depths will be slow, bladderwrack and sea lettuce winding around my ankles. The current will start to take me off my feet. My clothes will drag me down. I will let go and let the ocean take me.

Old Joe teetered to the left, travelling so slowly on his bike he defied gravity. He parked up and I joined him on the bench, closer to the sea but still on the way to the meeting room. He ate a small bag of chips. I listened as his gums masticated the chips, softened by the malt vinegar. He peeled the batter from his sausage and sucked on the golden pieces until they melted in his mouth. He nibbled at the pink sausage meat, making it last. His fisherman's cottage is in such poor condition it ranks one up from squalor. He straps his coat closed with a belt of rope. He used to live with his brother. A pair of aging bachelors. When the brother died, he left Joe alone. I walked away too and entered the meeting room five minutes after the session had started, avoiding the awkward small talk as each patient grabbed weak Nescafe with small cups of UHT milk which would taint the already mediocre coffee. The rich tea biscuits didn't help entice me in either.

I look at my last few notes.

> *Old Joe out cycling again today.*
> *Malcolm walks his dog 6pm.*
> *No sign of Hugh.*

Nothing personal. The date pencilled in at the top of the page looks interchangeable. Erasable. I try to read another page or two of my book. The brother in it is a useless buffoon who does nothing to support his ailing mother. A few Christmases ago, Jake wanted a brother, more than he wanted a Nintendo Switch; he had now come to terms with the fact getting one seemed unlikely with his dad living in a different house and his mother's eggs dry and shrivelled. He focussed on getting a new games console after that.

Some parents have babies to harvest their stem cells. Science enabling God-like acts to save siblings. If Jake has a disease, I have already left it too late. My reproducing days are over. I would also be unable to fund the stem cell harvesting. When he was born it cost more than a thousand pounds to cryogenically freeze a potential cure for any future illnesses. Maternity pay is not calculated to future proof your new family.

I shake away the injustice of the world.

Slumping deeper into my mattress, my eyes water and my jaw aches as my face stretches out a yawn. Tonight sleep teases me. My heavy eyes pull downwards. The wind, the turbines, the waves all seem to quieten for me. I push my hands under my bum to warm them through. Salty tears catch in the wrinkle of my top lip before spilling over into my mouth. I lick them away and push my damp face into the pillow.

24 Days

23:15

The snooty tone of the school's attendance officer will not stop pulsing through my head. *Good morning Mrs Farrington. We are just phoning to see where Jake is this morning. Is he ill?*

Ermm. Yes. Diarrhoea and sickness again I'm afraid.

Well, I'm sure you already know the forty-eight hour rule, yes?

When he stays home, I can keep him safe. No accidents. No run-ins with psychos. I'd watched Malcolm come back from his weekly Tesco shop this morning. He stood at the end of his block-paved drive, one of those new neat ones that cause flash-flooding in suburbia, and stared at our house. The blinds were closed to protect Jake's eyes from unnecessary stimulation and to avoid his headache progressing to a migraine. As an added bonus the darkened room helped me manage an afternoon nap. Through a small gap — thanks to Dave's ill-fitting blinds — I kept an eye on Malcolm as he studied our house. His eyes bored holes through Jake's window. Was he drawn to the blind because the pattern of galaxies and planets appealed to him? I bought it because I loved the way it shut out the light but simultaneously it brought in the magic of the universe. Or did Malcolm have another reason for staring at Jake's window the longest? If it wasn't Malcolm checking up on Jake, it was the school.

The attendance officer did have her uses though. I wince at the impulsiveness of my decision today.

Oh I'm glad you rang. My husband changed his mobile number and wanted me to tell you his new contact details.

Oh okay. Hold on a moment and I'll bring up Jake's records on screen so we can edit them. Okay, I've got them here. Is it his mobile that's changed?

Yes.

What's the new number? The number appeared in my head, all the digits blinking in a digital light display. A combination of birthdays and anniversaries.

Zero-seven-three-five-six-seven-one-two-nine-double zero.

Dave hadn't been in touch yet so didn't deserve to be on the emergency contact list any more. And he won't get a phone call if Jake is absent either.

Jake ate his lunch stationed in front of the TV; the lounge in semi-darkness too. He watched Dave's favourite film, *Back to the Future*. I left the room, frightened he might start asking after his dad. How can I explain why he never bothers to ring? Should I tell him his own dad isn't worth the heart ache? Jake's disappointment in his dad affects me too. His devastation spreading to me by osmosis. His pain writhing in my stomach like indigestible stones. While he dipped his soldiers in his runny egg, I snuck upstairs and changed Dave's number in his mobile too, so that he couldn't call his dad on a whim. He had been too angry with him since he left, but he might change his mind if Marty McFly and Biff make him yearn for him. The pain spreads from my stomach to my chest, labouring my breathing.

We'll see Jake Friday then, the attendance officer sounded so sure.

I sway with the thought of letting Jake leave the house. I steady myself by placing my palm on the wall. Damp plaster chills my fingertips. I shut out the thought. I cannot contemplate anything beyond the horizon of today.

23:47

I can't shift the penetrative cold in my hands and feet, no matter how many times I wrap them in my duvet or place them between my warm thighs. I swing my legs out the bed and go to locate the thermostat.

I find it by the fan heater at the back of the kitchen, where the radiator's warmth can never reach. Jake must have been fiddling with it. It says it's fifteen degrees but it feels sub-ten. I take it with me upstairs clicking the left button several times until the flame appears on the display. Digging around in my drawers, I pull out warm socks, the ones with a fleece lining, and slip them on my feet. The soft lilac knitted throw that normally frames the end of the bed goes around my shoulders and I turn on the lamp for a warm orange glow. Pulling out my journal, I start to add to my list of observations for the day.

> *11.15ish Malcolm being nosey again. Feigned watering his plants in the porch but definitely looking in Jake's window.*
> *Still only one car across the road. No sign of Hugh.*
> *Leanne has been going to work as usual.*

I close it and put it back in the drawer.

A crow or a raven or maybe it's a jackdaw, squawks outside. I once looked up which was which, but I can't remember the details tonight. One has a grey beak, I know that, but I have no idea which one. The bird aims his loud complaint at me. My bird-feeder swings emptily, taunting the local birds. When I had put mealworms out to attract the robins, the starlings ate them all. The blackbirds didn't get a look in either so I stopped putting them out. I might try again with some sort of device that restricts the feeding to smaller birds, the ones who need my help. The squawking stops.

There are no noises at all.

Not even Jake. He hasn't kicked the wall or snorted his little pig snuffle since I came to bed. I go and check on him. Earlier I had pulled my socks up to my knees and now I slide them down so that my pyjama shorts and socks combo doesn't look quite so ridiculous. As if the fashion police are spying on me in the early hours of the morning. I don't want to freak Jake out if he wakes. But I need to hear him breathing.

I pad across the room, the fleece lining of my socks cushioning my steps.

Once at Jake's door, I nudge it a few millimetres at a time to avoid the creak. It doesn't work. The noise startles him and his hands rush to his eyes, rubbing to try and clear his vision.

'Sorry, Jake. Didn't mean to wake you.'

'Mum?'

'Go back to sleep. Sorry.'

'You okay?'

'All good. Go back to sleep.' I back out the room. 'Sorry.'

23 Days

01:37

Several hours after tucking Jake in, I am still watching back-to-back episodes of *Homes under the Hammer*. How many episodes are there? The desire to reorganise my bedroom layout to maximise the view from my bed grows inside me with every episode. If I angled the bed slightly to the left, I could have a sea view with my morning coffee. A minor one, and the jaunty angle might seem contradictory to the usual 'bed against the wall tradition', but perhaps worth the compromise if I can glimpse the horizon. I measure out the size of the bed by laying my feet heel to toe and counting out the steps. In my rough estimation, I would be a big toe short of space meaning the upheaval would likely be unsuccessful. I let the disappointment roll off my shoulders. I don't need the hassle anyway.

I stop by the window. The full moon hangs like a light bulb, illuminating our unadopted road with its muted glow. The majestic sky, with deep purple hues reflects off the sea and I wonder how the world can carry on looking beautiful when so many bad things happen every day.

Jake will have to go back to school tomorrow.

Today, during the school's 'check-in call', the attendance officer suggested a meeting: *a reintegration meeting.* I recognised the lingo and knew what it meant. They are concerned about his absences. They want to question him, and me. They know about my mental health issues, the attendance officer raised it more than once in our brief conversation, her tone equally patronising and sympathetic. I shut her down with curt replies. I tried to suggest a reintegration meeting would be unnecessary. Intrusive even. They ignored me and made the appointment anyway.

Voices of my ex-colleagues chase their way through my head, inundating Jake with questions about me. *How is Mum, Jake? Anything we can do? Is Dad helping?* I scratch my scalp, trying to scrape the words away but they echo in my skull. Scrambling around in the bedside table, I pull out my bottle of pills and fight the child lock. I empty two capsules into the palm of my hand. I hesitate. How long has it been since I last medicated? It's probably not my usual fortnight but I need them. Tipping out three, I gulp them down with yesterday's water. The tablets stick in my throat so I swallow again until the lump passes. I close my eyes and vow I will keep a better record of my usage going forward.

22 Days

01:55

Still no sign of Hugh.
Malcolm asked about Jake today.

My pen nib catches on the grains woven into the coarse paper of my notebook. The parchment pages, worthy of a monk or an ancient philosopher, had been a gift from my mum. She had discovered it in a charity shop and thought it too good to leave behind. I add an exclamation mark to my notes about Malcolm. What a cheek.

He popped round, *to check on us*. Or so he claimed.

Has Jake been ill?

Despite wanting to shut the door in his face, I filled him in on Jake's minor ailments — headaches and stomach bugs. *You know what kids are like.*

I noticed your blinds have been closed a lot.

What did he think we were doing? I'm not some secret-keeping spy or vampiric mum turning each resident of Sheppey, one at a time, until it becomes the Isle of the Undead. I chuckled at my internalised joke and Malcolm looked at me like I reminded him of a deranged inmate of Bedlam.

I love vampire movies. Especially *The Lost Boys*. Kiefer Sutherland's creepy voice. The noodles switching to maggots; the bottle of wine to blood. I shudder with the memory of my childhood fear as Corey Haim sang in the bathtub. Waiting for the jump scare. Tame compared to today's TV. The Mind Flayer in *Stranger Things* freaked me out with its bubbling flesh melding into a grotesque beast. I shut my eyes. Opening them only when the image dissolves. As I turn on my pendant lamp, floods of light bleach the grey and lemon walls to a sterile white. They are safe and clean.

I decided to keep Jake home again today because he looked like he needed some mummy love. You know the kind of TLC no one else can give. And what was the point of him going in for a Friday. Surprisingly, Jake took some convincing.

Anyway why did Malcolm even notice, or care, about Jake's attendance at school? No good reason springs to mind.

Next time I will leave the blinds open and stay in the back room, away from prying eyes or maybe get off the island for the day instead. *A change is as good as a holiday,* Mum always says that. I wonder where she is docking next. I imagine her waddling down the platform in her new Clark's sandals at her own pace. *I need to be comfy, Vivian.* Her straw hat pulled down over the delicate skin on her ears. *I might be the next Shirley Valentine. You should've sent Jake to his dad's and come with me!*

I wish she would ring. Maybe I should plug the landline back in. The attendance officer won't be calling at this time of day.

Instead of closing the blinds, I could buy some of that hazed sticky film for my windows to obscure Malcolm's view. I type sticky film into my phone and skim the results for Amazon's Choice. With my order placed, I check my phone for the confirmation email. Ten unopened messages blink at me, most being unwanted sales notifications from Oliver Bonas and Toast. Brands I can no longer afford, even at sale prices. A new clairvoyant, Madame Enderby, *call me Mavis,* has sent over an email with her postcode details. Is that appointment tomorrow? I had found her online and booked an appointment one afternoon during a sleep-deprived stupor. The website had mentioned she was affiliated with the Spiritual Society in Sheerness. I had booked a private reading to avoid a crowded room of emotional women. I bring up Google Maps and the pin shows me a flat on the seafront. Jake can play the Xbox while I am gone. I must remind him to keep the blinds closed in the front of the house though, until the sticky film arrives. And to keep the windows shut too. I'll leave via the back door and out the side gate to avoid the neighbours knowing I have left Jake alone. Even alone, home is the safest place for him, but it's better if nosey Malcolm doesn't know I'm gone.

I scroll through Madame Enderby's website looking for tips on how to get the most from my session. It says I need something personal that belonged to the relative who I would like to make contact with. Should I take something of my late grandmother's, my uncle's or my father's? Do my relatives watch me with Jake from the other side? Do they question my parenting skills like the school, or do they understand? Do they sense my fear? Do they know what his premonition means? What is going to happen to him? I close my eyes and remember family dinners. Sunday roasts with trays of Yorkshire puddings, the middles bubbled up and their sides reaching skywards. Crisp and golden brown, yet soft and doughy in the middle. The beef gravy, rich and aromatic, swelling to the edges of the patterned crockery. Desserts, always shop-bought Vienetta or Arctic Roll, presented on silver platters as if they were masterpieces. Will they tell me what might happen to Jake? Will they help me?

I roll over and flick on the bedside light. 03:14. Sleep refuses to take me. I pick up my phone, touch the Facebook app and start to scroll.

21 Days

I flick through my scribbled notes from Madam Enderby's reading and cannot find one thing she said that can be construed as a sign that tragedy will strike. And despite dragging out my grandmother's embroidered handkerchief and my dad's tiepin from the bottom of my odds and sods drawer, there was no contact from my dead loved ones either. Neither of them. I guess I will return them to the drawer with the selection of USB cables and dried-up pens; they're about as much use. All Madam Enderby offered me was a confusing message that could have been meant for my cousin but looking back at my notes I am not sure that makes any sense either. She moved off the island years ago and I have not seen her since. Even though nothing in my notes worries me, for which I am grateful, nothing has eased the waves of anxiety crippling me either. I can hear Dave laughing. Doubling over with incredulity that a fortune teller might be able to predict my future. That visiting a 'gypsy' could help me. *Charlatans, all of them.* Dave's response after my first visit to a clairvoyant echoes in my head. Is he right? Have I wasted fifty quid on a reading I can ill afford?

Perching on the end of my bed, I feel like a crow resting on a gravestone, staring into the dark cemetery beyond. A portent of danger. Malcolm's security light springs to life. On and off. On and off. Reflections appear and disappear in the puddles accumulated in the potholes. Something passes my eye line, but I miss it. I lean in and scan the expanse of black glass. Another flutter. I move closer. A brown moth hits the window, right between my eyes. I spring back. The moth's wings patter on the glass as it reaches for my pendant light. A tapping drum beat; the innocent insect must be concussed. Eventually, it flies towards Malcolm's security light. Smudge follows suit, trespassing across my neighbour's property without an inkling of shame, domesticated but unable to stifle his primal desire to hunt at night.

Is my insomnia primal too?

Does my mind keep me awake for evolutionary reasons? To check on my young. To keep him safe? All I want is to keep Jake safe.

I can call for his test results on Monday. After two o'clock. Jake will be at school. Unless he wants to stay off for one more day? In case it's something serious. If it's not, we can breathe a sigh of relief together and stop our collective worrying. What's the collective noun for worriers? A contagion of worry?

But if there's nothing wrong, where does that leave his prophecy? What does it mean?

Should I dismiss it?

If it's not an illness, could it be an accident? Accidents are common. Statistically more likely than a disease? I could Google it to find out. There's a risk that the results will give me something else to worry about but what if they're reassuring? Sod it. I stop procrastinating (Phil will be pleased) and type into my phone – what is the most likely cause of death for an eleven-year-old?

An immediate response to my morbid enquiry appears on the screen. I try to remind myself these are statistics and not to be a neurotic parent.

Road traffic accidents 20%

Fire arms 15%

Clearly the statistics are for the USA. I add UK to my search criteria.

Cancers replace guns. Our roads and our gun laws keep our kids safer than their American counterparts.

A site offering worldwide teenage mortality rates sits third on the list of search results. I click the link.

Girls: HIV/Aids, road traffic accident, lower respiratory infections, diarrhoea diseases, malaria.

Boys: Road traffic accidents, drowning, HIV/Aids, lower respiratory infections, diarrhoea diseases.

My proximity to the sea, and the mention of drowning makes me uncomfortable. Diarrhoea diseases remind me of Jake's bowel problems. His impending test results. I close my phone case to shut the words out.

I dismiss the thought of road traffic accidents and drownings with a vigorous shake of my head. My thoughts flutter like the moth at my window, tapping the inside of my skull. I push thoughts of diseases out of my mind too. There are no tropical diseases or fatal bacteria on this island. Not for years.

I play out how tomorrow's phone call might go instead. The sympathetic tone the receptionist will use to put me at ease and the way she will soften her voice as she breaks the news.

Is that Mrs Farrington?

Ms Farrington. Yes, it is.

We were wondering if we could make an appointment for you and Jake to see the doctor about his test results. Are you available tomorrow morning?

A face-to-face conversation will suggest bad news.

I screw up my face and try to replace the imaginary phone call with one that has a better outcome.

The crunch of gravel under wide tyres stops the cycle in my head.

I sit up and check the clock. 23:23. Leaning forward into the glass, I cup my hands around my eyes and peer into the darkness.

Hugh's back.

He pulls a large holdall from the boot and approaches the door. His hand hovers near the lock but before he can turn it, the door opens. Leanne stands in the aperture, filling it despite her small frame. They stare at each other like rival cats, backs arched, hair standing on end. The awkward tension travels through my window. The silence hangs between them before Leanne steps back to break it and lets him in. Hugh drops his holdall at her feet and she closes the door behind them.

The moth passes the window again. Missing the glass this time.

I sit on the bed and let myself fall backwards. How many times had I imagined the conversation I would have with Dave if he turned up on my doorstep, begging to return? My mind used to pivot between slamming the door in his face, silent admittance and a euphoric reunion.

I pick up my phone and the traffic accidents and drownings stare back at me. Do 10-14-year-old boys take more risks than the same-aged girls? My boy cousins once brought home a World War II bomb from a scrapyard near their house. Someone always told the story at family gatherings. Who carried it; how it bounced along the path. Both of them oblivious to the risks they faced. I'd never done anything like that. Drownings and road traffic accidents were dramatic statistics but Jake's imminent school trip to France includes some coastal erosion studies and wild swimming. Never mind the coach journey and ferry to get there. So many risks. If his test results do come back clear, we still have his school trip to navigate before his birthday. Anything could happen between now and then.

I can hear Phil clearing his throat. Like he always does before saying something he's said more than once (or twice). *One step at a time, Vivian. Try a hot drink. Blowing the drink can regulate your breathing.*

I placed my mug on the bedside table and now a skin of congealed milk covers the tepid drink. I fish it off with my fingernail and drag it to the edge of the cup, drinking the lukewarm malted milk concoction and swallowing two blue capsules with it. I crawl under the covers and curl into myself. What did we do so wrong that meant Dave didn't love us enough to stay? Will he even care if we are gone?

01:13

My blue capsules are slow to release their magic; the stress of Jake's blood test results curbing their effectiveness. I reach for the bottle and click the lid over and over again, until I get the pressure point right. I take an extra one, washing it down with another mouthful of my cold drink, the powdery residue at the bottom of the mug making my mouth feel like dry sand. I wiggle my tongue around my mouth to dislodge it. Straightening myself into a long, stretched out pose to relax my limbs, I wait for my pills to work.

20 Days

23:51

Trying to re-read the same sentence of my novel for the fourth time, I'm careful not to disturb the sleep that might be close. I turn the book face down and rest it on my knee. I keep my movements small so I don't scare the sensation away.

Until I pestered Jake about his mood, the house had oozed a funereal quiet this morning. Rather unlike his placid nature, when I questioned him he had exploded and refused to say one word about the dark cloud that had followed him around since he had woken up. His silence grew stronger, so I pushed harder. He spilled his confession along with a barrage of tears. He had been grilled online by Logan's mum about his continued absences from school. Whilst he tried to play Fortnite, and disappear into an imaginary world, she had interrupted their game and probed him for gossip.

I raged inside. She'd texted me already. I'd ignored her interfering questions. She'd rang me instead of taking the hint.

The reverberation of her fake jollity still resounded in my ears. Her questions hidden under the veil of concern, *Is everything alright at home, Vivian?* When I hung up, I unplugged the land line again. So she'd tried Jake. What right had she to interfere in our lives?

Once calmed down and installed on his Xbox, I tried to quiz him further. Aiming my delivery of questions between intricate moves, each plea punctuated by the artillery fire of virtual weapons in his bedroom. He wouldn't let my words squeeze between the relentless chatter and gun fire. How many eleven-year-olds had been listening to our conversation? I had watched my words but the sudden thought that other parents might have been listening too, struck me like a slap. I hope that Logan's mum, the interfering cow, had been listening so she could hear what I really thought of her. Gaming consoles are like spies in your home. Jake had barely shared a thing between his battle calls. *Cover me. Collect that weapon. Get it. Now. Quick. Yes!*

Without Jake's version of events, Logan's mum's voice squeaks and whispers and pushes around inside my head. An archaeologist mining Jake for information.

Jake, why were you off school again?

Mum said I wasn't well enough.

Were you?

Well, Mum said...

Yes, but what do you think?

Well yeah, I suppose.

And how is Mum?

Different versions of the same conversation circle me like birds of prey. Vultures. The room starts to spin. My intestines churn. My paperback slides from my knee; my page is lost. I run to the bathroom and retch over the toilet bowl. Nothing but bile and sleepy tea spills from my lips. Herbier and more acidic as it travels in reverse.

I check on Jake on my way back to bed. His limbs fill his single mattress. A foot pokes out of his quilt. Fish tank bubbles splutter behind me, a reminder that the tank needs cleaning. Next to his bed, the small patch of mould where his mattress meets the wall looks bigger than the last time I inspected it. Are the black marks multiplying? I place my palm against it and feel the damp plaster on my fingers. A couple of smoky spores smear across the wall. Dave promised he would sort it out this summer, when the weather would help to dry it out. Well, that's not happening now.

Jake's phone vibrates and blue light fills the room as a notification arrives. I try to smother the sound with my over-sized sleeve. He had asked to call his dad earlier. *It's too late honey. Maybe tomorrow.* Another notification pops up but I realise now it is set to silent. *He's such a good boy.* My mum often says this as though she expects my son to be a monster. I punch in his passcode. A close up of Smudge's smudge, a giant grey splodge on top of his head, fills the screen. I scroll through Jake's notifications. There's a missed call from an unknown number. Three hours ago.

It's Dave's mobile, no longer stored in his contacts.

He wouldn't have been in bed long when it rang. Typical of Dave to ignore the fact he would be in bed by nine. I discard the notification. Dave will quiz him and Jake will innocently reveal I haven't returned to work or that he has been off school. I slide past the apps until I reach the settings icon. I hesitate.

'Don't interfere, Vivian.' My voice sounds stern in his quiet room but it's easy to ignore your own orders. I tell myself interfering, when it is for the greater good, is okay. I click on recent calls and find Dave's number. I hit block caller. The phone vibrates in my hand. I drop it.

The thud as it hits his new carpet, something I wish I could afford for my own room, makes Jake's mouth drop open and his breathing falter. He rolls over and settles again. I pick his phone back up, ignoring the notification from Jamiecakeface who should be asleep at this time of night, and place it back on the desk, face down.

Returning to my room, I pick up my book and flick through to find my page. Maud's broken mind feels too distressing to read about tonight and the mystery of her missing sister too convoluted for me to follow. I abandon the book again. Reading requires more focus than I am capable of right now.

00:13

I look down at the three tablets sticking to my sweaty palm. If I take them, it will be the second night in a row. But the innocuous blue pills do help. If I don't take them, Jake's looming test results will spin around my head in a continuous swirl like the fossilised shells on Jake's windowsill. One more night and then I will have a break from them.

I place the tacky pills on my tongue and close my mouth, pushing them down with saliva alone.

19 Days

21:19

There are no concerns at all Mrs Farrington.

What about the blood?

Probably mild constipation. Get him to take the fibre drink daily, add to that a probiotic drink like the doctor suggested and keep his fluid intake up. And his vegetable intake too, if at all possible. The nurse's smile came through the line with her words. She must have a fussy eater too. *We realise it can be tricky.*

The relief was fleeting. The escalation to worrying about Jake's school trip came so quickly it unbalanced me. I lowered myself down to the kitchen stool, steadying myself with the table edge. Why should I be one of the lucky ones? One of the ones whose child doesn't suffer some terrible illness. Someone whose child doesn't die. To believe it won't happen to me suggests I am worthy of some special treatment by fate.

I'm not.

I don't deserve special treatment.

I don't give to the homeless outside Tesco. I avoid eye contact on purpose, afraid to be duped by frauds who go home to their houses that probably have better central heating than mine. I fast-forward the sad stories featured on *Children In Need* so I don't have to feel their pain. I don't deserve for bad luck to bypass me and find someone else. In all likelihood the prophecy is true. And I probably deserve it. My first pregnancy. The one that didn't take. There were reasons for that. My drinking and partying. My uninhabitable womb. Guilt swims inside me.

All normal, Mrs Farrington.

Nothing to worry about Mrs Farrington.

Ms Farrington, I hear myself say. As if that is of any importance.

Accidents can kill.

I had bookmarked the Google search results and know the statistics by heart. Thinking of the numbers triggers a pain in my chest. My insides short circuit until it hampers my breathing. I suck in and out. *Smell the soup; cool the soup, Vivian.*

I pick up my book and breathe out slowly as I turn the page and read each individual word aloud, like I'm back to sounding out each phoneme with Jake. At the start of the page a man is eating but I don't remember him entering a restaurant or ordering food. I flick back a page and it's there, the dining club and the luncheon. Broth and stewed plums on the menu. Not able to follow the story I continue to pronounce each syllable out loud.

It brings no relief from the chaos in my head.

Reading used to help.

I move my tongue around my mouth, stretching and manipulating the muscles in my face, forcing it to relax. I direct every breath through my nose and back out my mouth in the vague memory of yoga breathing exercises that connect the physical to the spiritual. Stretching my eyes wide, they sting with exposure to the air. My tongue, swollen with mouth ulcers, feels too large for the gap between my teeth and the build-up of plaque on my lower teeth scratches at it as it pushes up against them.

Accidents kill.

The terror builds despite my best efforts to push it out with my deep breathing. It poisons me. Erodes my sanity.

'Trust your instincts, Vivian.'

The doctors and nurses cannot possibly know from a five-minute session what is or isn't wrong with my son. Talking to myself may make my sanity questionable but I must trust my gut.

And accidents cannot be predicted.

I chew the inside of my cheeks, wiggling my jaw as my flesh gradually makes its way out from between my molars. Firm enough to feel it but not enough to bleed.

It could be an accident on the walk to school. Some incident on the school trip to France. He leaves in two weeks. I remember Zeebrugge. Watching the news when the *MS Herald of Free Enterprise* capsized. My mind flicks to training sessions at work and horrific tales of students dying on school trips. Falling off the rapids at theme parks, drowning whilst kayaking. Despite the risk assessments, teacher supervision and other professionals being on hand, accidents continue to happen on school trips. Why would he be immune?

I'll stay on the sofa tonight. No point in pretending I might sleep.

Jake reacted to the doctor's all clear announcement with a celebratory can of Dr Pepper and a packet of plain Walker's crisps. His rubbish still decorates the lounge floor. Relief had washed over him as he munched through his reward. His shoulders dropped an inch.

I faked happiness for him. Held my smile in place as crumbs gathered around his lips.

I wipe salt from the empty crisp packet, using my finger to hold it on my mouth ulcer. My jaw tenses with the instant pain. The ulcer shrinks as the salt sucks moisture from my mouth.

I pick up the can and help myself to his leftovers. Earlier, the spicy fizz of his Dr Pepper had sprinkled my nose as I leant in to kiss him. *Restores vim, vigour and vitality.* I had repeated the old slogan in a jolly voice. He laughed.

The fizz is all gone. Syrup fills my mouth. Fear fills my head instead of bubbles. I swallow and tilt my head left, then right. The muscles in my neck strain with the effort, tight like a rope under the weight of its acrobat. A fine balance between safety and catastrophe. Keeping Jake home will ensure that nothing can happen to him. He must not go to France. School is risky enough.

I will lie to him.

Tell him school has flooded or there has been an electrical fault which means that school has to close for a few days. If I keep him home with the Wi-Fi off, he will never know. We can play games. Scrabble and full-length Monopoly. Not that shortened card game my mum bought him to save her own sanity. He loves card games too: gin rummy and twenty-one. We will use matchsticks for stakes. Maybe I could teach him poker, if I can remember the hands and their values. Chess too. I will need to improve my game, as every match we play ends in stalemate.

I can keep him home until his birthday. Nineteen days. Doable. I need a plan.

I lean forward and grab my journal from the coffee table. It falls open on a blank page and I start to write. Ink haemorrhages into the new paper. I scratch through options. Untidy notes start to build into a plan. Organising my thoughts invigorates me and my body pulses with desire. I feel invincible. An orgasm would be an easy feat tonight, but I want to have sex again, not masturbate. It would take my mind off all this shit. I think of Hugh across the road and Leanne's pleas for forgiveness. Was she getting a double helping? Hugh's long hair, bohemian and well-groomed at the same time, suddenly appeals. My body starts to feel like it belongs to someone else. I need to feel something before the invisibility my mum talks about takes me too. Low moods. Itchy skin. Dryness. The swelling. The water retention. Will every symptom of menopause coming at me now continue until my redundant body withers into a shrunken shell?

My mind whirls like a hurricane pulling every element of my life into the storm. I'm in the eye and I want it to stop. The wind, the rain, every lightning strike, bring fear with them. I need to break the cycle. I need to see Jake.

I tiptoe upstairs. Jake sleeps on his front, mouth ajar, his audiobook playing. I top up his fish tank to stop the spluttering of the pump and turn off his book. His face, if carved in marble, could not be finer. I climb in next to him. He grumbles and rolls over. With the extra room, I curl myself around him, desperate to hold him. Sweat beads on his top lip. I kiss it and it melts into my skin.

Why would I waste time sleeping? I fold his hand in mine until it fits inside my fist. I stare at Jake's fish circling the tank and envy its limited mind and memory. Its ability to restart afresh every few seconds, no awareness of life's delicate balance. The goldfish weave, dive and ascend the tank as if exploring a vast ocean for the first time. As I straighten out my legs, Jake shuffles and leans into his teddy. I breathe in his sleeping body. If I can keep him home. It will be enough. It has to be.

18 Days

22:59

I trace the imprint of my watch on my wrist until I reach two parallel moles. I join them with a line and then drag my finger across towards a third. I realise I have not travelled between the moles with any order or logic so I start again. Tracking by size, I reach my upper arm and then divert to my armpit. I notice a mole so black that it looks like a pinhole camera, and decide to classify by colour instead. I start again. From pitch to muddy brown to a pale tan.

Thirteen moles. Finally, I reach my waist. Seventeen. I land on the mole that moved several inches during my pregnancy with Jake, never quite returning to the same point on my side. Forever displaced. Twenty-three. The next mole, under my breast, has a top that feels pickable. A crusty oval, no change to its shape for years but more grey than brown and with a definite lip that my nail tip is drawn to. My nail wants to nestle under the mole and wiggle the crusty top free. I stop myself in time. Twenty-seven moles on the front of my upper body. Two black pins, three large ovals — a deep chestnut in colour — and the scabby grey one, hidden amongst twenty-one other moles that form a constellation on my body. I've no one to check my back for abnormalities now. I reverse my path and re-join them with my trailing finger.

Counting moles makes a change from counting leaves on my wallpaper or sheep on my pyjamas but now the scabby mole bothers me. Each time I let my finger roam towards it, I imagine the scab coming off, the blood blossoming in its place and then my skin blistering. The vision worsens, with pustules oozing as if the removal of the scab has started a cancerous spread that will cover my whole body before morning. I climb out of bed and wash my hands, trying to let the thought of the scabby mole travel down the plughole with the water.

I check Jake's toothbrush. Damp. Good, that means I didn't forget the basics tonight. He hadn't needed as much persuading to stay home today. I left him in bed until he woke naturally and made sure I rang the school before they rang me, telling them he'd had a bad night. *He won't be in today. He needs to recuperate.* I spoke with authority. He'd been annoyed with me when he woke and realised he'd missed registration but he admitted to feeling tired. He hates the extra attention of turning up late, so had no desire to arrive mid-lesson. One mention of checking his bowel movements, to ensure it wasn't too loose with the new medication they recommended to soften his stools, had him curled up on the sofa in front of the TV.

I disconnected the Wi-Fi to pull him away from *Young Sheldon* and claimed to report the fault on my app before suggesting that he play board games with me. They didn't hold his attention for long. Not like they had on camping holidays or over the Christmas break. Maybe two players made for a meagre game, curtailing his competitive spirit. Beating his Mum too easy a feat. The distraction of his Xbox, and a constant stream of YouTube videos of other teenagers playing their Xboxes appealed more than my chess skills. The thought of those kids holed-up in their bedrooms, manifesting RSI as they make a living out of gaming and stretching their parents' hospitality upsets me. Little boys want to be YouTubers now. Not train drivers. Not even footballers. By quarter past eleven, I had given up on holding his attention and turned the Wi-Fi back on, faking another message on my app to say it was fixed.

00:26

I look in the bathroom mirror and pull at the loose skin around my eyes. The sink gurgles as water circles the drain. I wipe my hands on the dry flannel and wonder when Jake last washed his face. At least he had brushed his teeth. One out of two: I'll take that as a parenting win. I mould the mangled tube of toothpaste back into shape.

Faint voices creep through the door. I push it open and see his mobile on the bedside table. David Baddiel's nasal voice narrating *Turbochaser* into the room. I pause Audible, unplug his phone and lean on the end of his bed. Cupping his hand inside mine until it disappears. All mine. Like when my pregnant belly protected him from the world and only I knew he was there.

00:34

A car door slams.

'No.'

I move closer to Jake's window.

'What do you mean, no?'

Earlier, Hugh and Leanne left, dressed for dinner in the way childless couples do. A make-up date? I had wondered if they'd choose a romantic meal at Banks in Minster or The Playa on the seafront famous for its mussels. The other choices on the island are limited, unless you want pub grub but that doesn't equate to make-up food. I haven't eaten out since being signed off work and wished it was me and Jake going for a slap-up meal. Socialising, or doing anything for pleasure while recuperating, and off work, brings a heap of guilt. Like bunking off school and getting caught in Woolworths filling a pick n mix bag. Phil claimed anything that aided my recovery should be embraced — even if that meant going on holiday. But I couldn't. And where could I afford to go? Leysdown? And what if someone from work saw me gallivanting about?

I peek behind Jake's planet blind. The small window opening barely wide enough to let air in let alone lean out of.

I need ventilation, Mum.

Safety first, Jake.

Leanne must have been drinking because she carries an unfinished bottle in one hand (red, so they'd probably been to Banks) and her handbag in the other. One of those over-sized, over-priced ones always hanging from the waif-like arms of celebrities in *OK* and *HELLO!* magazines. Their arms looking like they need a gym workout.

'I mean, no — I'm done with IVF. Hormone treatments. Alcohol-free, cigarette-free, fun-free months. Injecting you in the arse and putting up with your moods. I'm done.'

Conversation over. Hugh slams the car door and turns his back on Leanne. She staggers across the drive after him.

'Don't you want a family?'

'Not like this.'

I pull back from the window, embarrassed to have heard their private moment. I wander back to my own room and get in bed. Jake is here. In my house. In his bed. With no signs of anything being wrong with him. *A healthy young man, Mrs*

Farrington. I focus on being thankful. I have not tried a gratitude journal yet, despite Phil's tentative suggestions. Maybe I should.

00:44

Counting my fingers and my toes, one to twenty, I try to independently move each one each time. As I reach my final left pinky, I start again, determined to remember my healthy son. His wailing lungs. His ten fingers and ten toes. All in the room next door. Fit and well.

17 Days

In the distance, the relentless flow of rain mixes the sea to the sky. We've had enough rain today to summon an ark. The weather no longer knows what month it is, let alone what season. Autumn but with the power of summer storms behind it. I stand at the window watching another deluge make its way to the sill. The deep grooves in Hugh's gravel, left by the force of his SUV, fill with water again. He hasn't been back.

Leanne had opened her curtains briefly but soon closed them when dusk arrived. I kept mine closed after I spotted Malcolm's binocular lens glinting in the small bit of sunlight we'd seen all morning. I knew he claimed to be a twitcher; he'd talked to Dave about our sycamores which attracted a wider variety of birds compared to his row of conifers. He'd been nursing a sapling for the last eight years but despite his best efforts it remains a twiggy stem bending in the sea breeze. Malcolm encourages us to complete the RSPB survey every spring but no sooner do I spot a bird then it flies away and I am left looking at the identifying leaflet confused. A finch? A tit? A common sparrow? Paralysed by the fear of misleading the RSPB and their bird-loving followers, I never submit my findings.

Malcolm's lens intruded into our house more than once today. Not remotely embarrassed by being spotted, he waved, narrowing his eyes to focus on me through the lens. I nodded and gave him a pinched smile in an attempt to show my disgust. I then tugged the blind closed and shut him out.

Water splashes outside as a car crosses over drowned gravel. Beyond my bedroom blind, Hugh's car crunches into his driveway opposite. He jumps out and hammers on his new front door. It's one of those fancy composite ones that try to look like wood but when you touch them, they feel nothing like timber, despite the imprinted grain. No warmth to them with nature absent from their construction. Hugh hammers again. He's getting wet.

'Leanne.' I can hear his gritted teeth beneath his words. 'Let me in.'

A light illuminates their loft conversion. The large VELUX window glowing in the dark.

'Leanne, open the god-damn door.' His voice echoes in the street, bouncing off the wheelie bins lined up for tomorrow's collection. Leanne does not emerge. The hall light stays out.

She obviously isn't planning on coming down to see him. His fist strikes the letterbox with a thud and he grunts before shaking his hand with a wince. A hardwood door would have been even less forgiving. Did I put my bin out?

'It's my house too.' He starts to kick the bottom panel. Has she deadlocked it? Or had he left without his keys? He turns around. Strands of wet hair stick to his face. Has he given up? Will he leave her alone? He steps back, and switches course, running shoulder first, with every ounce of his weight behind him, into the door. His body jolts backwards and with a satisfying stumble he lands on his arse. I laugh while Hugh's anger escalates. He scrambles to his feet, brushing himself off and rattling the door handle.

'Answer the fucking door, Leanne.'

Rage pours out of his face. He steps into the beam of his headlights on his running car and they illuminate his burning cheeks which are glistening with rain. The VELUX window plunges back into darkness.

Hugh turns around and presses a button on his key fob. The BMW's boot opens gradually revealing light from within, like the door to an alien spaceship. He rummages around under the boot's carpet and pulls something out of the spare wheel bay.

Darkness hides his discovery from me. I squint to try and see through the murky night. He's back at the front door. The car's headlights bounce off steel. It's a crow bar he raises above his head.

'Shit.'

I fumble with the window latch. The hinges, rusted shut, squeak with the lift of the handle. As I push the window open, rain slides off Hugh's face.

'I don't think she's home.' I call out. Hugh wipes the rain from his face with one hand and lowers his weapon to his side, holding it behind his right leg. Thinking I haven't seen it.

'Oh right. Forgot my key — like an idiot.' His hand is shaking; his anger bleeds red patches into his neck. 'I'll just wait in the car. Thanks for that.'

'Prick.' I mutter under my breath. I step away from the window but watch from a distance as he throws the crowbar back into the boot and gets in the driver's seat. He drops his head to the steering wheel, leaving one foot hanging out of his open car door. His headlights highlight their landscaped driveway and potted topiaries. The interior light makes his white Nike trainers glow. I stand guard — worried Hugh might try to break in. I leave my window and blind open to aid my surveillance from my bed. The rain has almost stopped. I keep the bedside lamp off to improve my view outside. The crunch of his feet across the gravel will alert me to any movements outside but I will keep watch anyway. Poor Leanne. My eyes flit between Hugh, the VELUX window and Malcolm's house. Predators trying to catch their prey. The dark street and damp night seem to be absorbing all the usual night sounds. The air is heavy with silence. I ponder calling the police but don't want them asking questions. What if they interview Malcolm and he mentions Jake's been home from school? I will log what I have noticed so far this evening in my journal instead, in case Hugh does something stupid.

23:04

I have filled a page with the details of Hugh's return. I check him again; his head hasn't moved from its position on the steering wheel. It's been over nineteen minutes. An odd fluttering sound, which could be an owl or could be Hugh snoring whilst he sleeps off his anger, seeps into my room. An almost snore. I can't be sure it isn't Smudge in the spare room. I decide to risk making a cup of tea. I'd hear Leanne scream if something was wrong. A weak tea won't hurt at this time of night and with all the adrenaline pumping, thanks to Hugh, sleep is distant anyway. Dave liked strong tea — leave the bag in method. Disgusting. Teabags are designed to be squeezed and removed not left in while you drink. Some of my mugs still bear the stains of his over-stewed brews. He had taken the cycling memorabilia mug with him but left behind the Best Dad mug Jake had given him several Father's Days ago. I put a tea bag in the mug. It does have a stupid novelty handle shaped like

170

a trophy arm that even I can't get my fingers and knuckles through without scalding them on hot ceramic or spilt tea, but still, he could have taken it with him, shown some appreciation even if he didn't use it. I'd seen Jake's face crumple when he spotted it hanging on the mug tree the day after he left. I stir my tea until the liquid whirlpools; a habit left over from when I took two sugars. When flinging the teabag into the compost bin on the kitchen side, and chucking the teaspoon in the sink, I realise the drain stinks. I will bleach it tomorrow. I need to get back to my post.

01:07

No Smudge on the stairs or in the spare room. I pause at Jake's door. The breeze must have pushed it closed. Releasing the catch will risk waking him. I don't want to disturb his sleep. I go back to Hugh and Leanne instead.

Hugh acts as if he is under a spell. Or drunk? I wish I could cast my own spell and bind him to the seat to be certain he won't attack Leanne. Then *I* could lie down. I might not be able to sleep but resting comes a close second.

03:19

Hugh must be asleep. I haven't checked Jake in a while so pop to his room. When I open his door it creaks louder than usual despite my best efforts to ease it open. I go to the edge of his bed and rest my hand on his neck. Underneath my fingertips, I feel his blood pumping. His pulse flutters and touches my skin like the wings of a butterfly. His breathing changes for a few seconds. Stronger, heavier. Then it lulls as deep sleep returns to take him.

04:11

I am falling, catapulting forward into nothingness. A hypnic jerk jolts me towards wakefulness before sleep can take me.

My heart races with the shock of the imaginary fall.

I resist the urge to turn the bedside lamp back on and get up to check on Hugh. His car door remains open as if he's mid-escape, his high-tops glowing under the BMW's interior light. The haze of dawn is filling the sky. Morning feels close; I may as well get up.

16 Days

22:48

I am waiting on the edge of my bed for the neighbours'
nocturnal battle to re-start and the last twenty-four hours are
whirling around me like the sea mist blending with the grey
clouds on the horizon. I'm not sure how long I have been sat
here.

Did Jake go to school this morning?

The only thing I am certain of is that Hugh's SUV hasn't
moved. The crowbar disappeared hours ago and his front
garden, a perfect suburban design with a turning point cut into
the lawn, looks dry despite the recent rain. At the patchwork
lines of the turf, the edges are beginning to brown because they
have failed to follow the watering instructions. I worked in a
garden centre the summer after my GCSEs and still remember
that grass seed would have been an easier option. Cheaper, too.
But probably not instant enough for Insta.

Leanne must also be at home. Hugh's large BMW still blocks

in her diminutive Fiat 125. A retro throwback that I fawn over every time I get in my Ford Ka. My stupid vehicle with the stupid name that no one knows how to pronounce without looking pretentious. The Tango red paint is now so flat it resembles an old brick. I curse its temperamental electric windows and the bubbles of rust lining the wheel arches. The stereo cassette player remains its flashiest feature.

Despite Hugh and Leanne both being home there have been no fireworks so far but tempers always rise at this time of night in my experience. When the chores of the day are out of the way, evenings leave space for conflict.

I check my emails on my phone. An unopened one from Jake's school blinks back at me. I click on the closed envelope. I hadn't been able to face opening it earlier. My face flushes as I realise it is from a support worker updating me on Jake's reintegration today. Was I supposed to be there? The email informs me it went well.

He had been to school then.

Was it this morning I made sure he drank his probiotic yoghurt before he left? The support worker confirms she ensured he drank plenty of fluids in the day as requested.

Did I make sure he drank his fibrous drink before dinner? The synthetic lemon and lime flavoured powder thickens the water and makes him gag so he would have dodged it if he could have. I can't remember. A memory of him chasing it with a glass of squash pops into my head but that could have been yesterday. Or the day before. I can hear him complaining about it. Was that today?

I know, I can read the notes he keeps on his pad. In the bathroom I scan through his 'toilet' and 'diet' diary.

His bowel movements are regular but not as regular as they were. The streaks of blood are becoming less common but not any less significant for Jake. Every time that red line appears on the tissue, horror floods his face. Blood should be inside his body, under his skin, not showing itself to him, reminding him something must be wrong. I keep trying to reassure him. His response frightens me more than the blood itself; his unyielding conviction that he is afflicted by some serious ailment. We keep following the doctor's instructions. At home, I can remind him to drink regularly but the attendance officer has assured me that they can do that too. *You mustn't worry,* she said, as if parents come with an on-off switch to avoid the trauma of worry whenever it becomes inconvenient. How I wish that were true.

23:01

I return to the window. My eyes scan the neighbour's house for movement. The lights are still out in the loft's VELUX window. Hugh must be downstairs, watching an action movie if all the

175

flashing lights in the lounge window are anything to go by. Is Leanne watching it with him? I used to watch action movies with Dave but at some point I stopped pretending to like them and then I stopped tolerating them altogether. Why anyone would watch violence for entertainment baffles me; there is enough cruelty in the world without the film industry glamourising it. *Viv, it's just a bit of fun. Chill.* Dave refused to watch my period dramas, so there was no way I would waste my time watching *Die Hard 5* or 6 or whatever number they were on. The one programme we could all watch together, without anyone being offended or bored, was *Antiques Roadshow.* Jake loved it when someone brought along an ugly piece of pottery or garish jewellery and the expert announced it was worthless. Even better if it had gone down in value since they had purchased it. I wondered if this revealed a fault in his personality. Could you tell if someone would turn into a sociopath or a psychopath by examining their early TV proclivities?

Their joy in others' misfortunes?

I blame Dave. He rejoiced when other people failed too.

The flash of the crowbar flicks into my head. Was it still in the boot of the BMW or did Hugh take it inside the house? I imagine Leanne's head with a crowbar-shaped hole in the temple. Blood and brain matter in her hair, running into her eyes. Fluid oozing from her ears. Laid under the VELUX window. Unconscious. Bubbles of blood mixing with saliva on her lips, growing and popping each time she attempts to breathe. Her crushed ribs straining. I try to push the images away. This is why I don't watch action movies. Maybe I should start to avoid crime dramas too.

I squeeze my eyes shut to crush the image.

23:30

My neck cracks and creaks as I stand and crane my neck to check on the rest of the street. There are no other lights apart from the intermittent flash of Malcolm's security light and that blue glow seeping through the shutters in Hugh's lounge. Every time Jake walks past Hugh's house, he admires the large flat-screen TV filling the space on the wall above their fireplace. I hanker over their modern fireplace with the large pebbles hidden behind a sheet of safety glass.

Is a crime drama unfolding on the TV while Hugh's wife fights for her life on the landing? In the bathtub? Her twisted limbs curled into the space at the bottom of the stairs? Does he step over her to go to bed, making sure he doesn't get any of her bodily fluids on his cashmere slippers? I have no idea if Hugh wears cashmere slippers but he looks like he can afford them.

I back away from the window. Lying down with my arms

and legs out wide in the shape of a starfish, I shake out each limb, trying to send my fears out into the room. *Let them go, these fears that hold you ransom, let them go.* 'Oh Phil, I wish I could.'

Pulling the duvet with me, I shuffle up to the headboard and listen for Jake against the wall. The only sound reaching me is the pump fighting the falling water level in his fish tank again. I swear the fish drink it. I won't sleep with that racket so I tiptoe to the bathroom, fill the jug and empty the cold water into the aquarium. The gold and black fish, Sushi, wriggles with the shock of the chilly addition to his tepid ocean. *Keep swimming,* I silently plead with the one fish left from the trio Jake started with. I do not want to explain a death in the family tomorrow.

His frantic swimming settles into a smooth rhythm as he circles the sunken ship and the ruined bridge in an endless loop. The cold-water shock treatment causing no permanent damage.

Jake's breathing, now audible over the silenced tank, adds a steady sound for me to follow. I count each beat, mirroring his relaxed breaths with my own, slowing myself down. I back out of the room and go to my own window and close the blind. Still counting the beats of my breath, I shut out Leanne, Hugh and Malcolm. *Jake,* my number one concern, echoes in my head.

Thoughts of Leanne try to creep back in. Maybe I should knock tomorrow and see if she's home. I'll need a pretence under which I can legitimately call. Neither Hugh nor Leanne bothered integrating with the street. Not exactly an anti-social pair but both failed to attend the Neighbourhood Watch Team meeting, even after a friendly request by Malcolm.

The heavy crowbar looked comfortable in Hugh's grip.

His knuckles whitened. His upper body tensed.

Was I wrong not to report it to the Neighbourhood Watch Team last night? Is there a duty to report a neighbour wielding a lethal weapon? Should I call the police?

No. I can't do it now; the police would want to interview me. They would question Jake. Judge me. *Why is he at home and not in school?* Not that it would be related to their investigation but they must always be on the lookout for suspicious activity. I don't want the police in my house. I have nothing to hide but as mum says, *Why invite the wolf in?*

Leanne could be resting. Hiding out and ignoring her husband. The fight will have shaken her up. If it was me, I would be giving Hugh the silent treatment for being an idiot. Hugh, in his cashmere slippers, doesn't seem like a dangerous man. Well he didn't until the crowbar incident. But how many times have I heard that proclamation of innocence on the true crime channel? Dave used to glue himself to the sofa when the true crime documentaries came on. I preferred those to action movies; the grim reality of the truth as opposed to the ridiculous premise of fiction.

Does a dangerous man live across the street from us?

If Jake's bowel troubles are not part of the prophecy, what if Hugh is? Or Malcolm? It could be something, or someone, on this very street that kills him. Perhaps the same thing that killed Matthew. What if something in his bedroom is toxic? Will it leak into his skin, his blood, his bones? I imagine doctors circling his bed unable to find the cause of his symptoms. Treating him like a pin cushion as they run every available test. Images of Hugh Laurie in his role in *House* spring to mind. Would they postulate over what could be slowly killing Jake? Would they tell me lies to appease me? To make me stop pleading with them to save my boy? Wasn't it always lupus? What is that? Could that be what is wrong with Jake? I get out of bed, shake my limbs harder than usual to release the tension but the image of the hospital bed, with men in white coats won't shift. I go downstairs and put the TV on. Repeats of *Homes Under the Hammer* wash over me as I cocoon myself in a blanket. The sound of the auction gavel and home renovations comfort me.

15 Days

Sushi circles the tank. Under the bridge, over the bridge, through the bridge. Different routes. Same destination. Over and over again.

My fingers are laced between Jake's. His damp and sweaty clasp, trying to convince me, despite the large amount of blood he found earlier in the evening, that his body thrives. It tells me that this is not what my catastrophising brain thinks it is. I close my eyes and pinch the bridge of my nose with my spare hand, holding my thoughts inside my head.

What did more blood mean? Was this an emergency? Should I take him to A&E? Jake had stood in front of me in his Lego pyjamas, the Stormtrooper filling his chest, making him look younger and reminding me of all the Christmas eves I've given him a new pair. The tissue in his hand showed me things are getting worse. We both knew it.

I close my eyes and Matthew appears in Jake's place. Pale

and broken. He loved Lego too and dusty models lined his shelves. When we viewed the house, he seemed like a quiet, shy boy, if a little displeased to find someone looking at his room with covetous eyes. I remember his mother saying, *Don't worry you'll have a bigger room in the new house.* Is it the room that affects Jake? The mould that is fighting its way back through the plaster? Is it a killer pulsing in the wall? My body jolts, knocking him as he sleeps.

'Mum?' Sleepy eyes peek from behind his long lashes.

'Sorry honey. Someone walked over my grave. That's all. Go back to sleep.' Was it Matthew?

Earlier I had tried my best to reassure him. *It is a little more but still a really small amount, babe. Flush that down the loo, wash your hands and get back to bed. Have you written it in the diary?* He nodded. *Ok, off you go then and I'll be up to tuck you in shortly.* I forced my best smile onto my face, glued it there with gritted teeth.

This blood was vibrant. A dangerous red. A colour to make you stop and notice. No longer does Jake's concern seem like an overreaction. Despite my best efforts to convince him that I do, I don't believe the innocuous statements of the doctors. I have read *Woman's Weekly* in the dentist's waiting room so I know doctors misdiagnose all the time. My worry about him won't stop, like the tide smashing a sea defence with relentless force it will carry on regardless. What would make my tide of worry ebb away? I wish I knew. Could my pregnancy blood test have come back skewed, not because of an extra chromosome, but because of some other defect. Something they didn't know to look for back then.

A couple more chapters of *Harry Potter* had soothed him eventually, and I read on until Harry defeated Peter Pettigrew and the Dementors. A little bit of hope against adversity to bolster his spirits. I held his hands, stroked his fingers, his neck. I combed his overgrown fringe with my fingers, releasing the scent of my shampoo in his hair. I kissed him on his head, his shoulders, his nose, again and again, wishing the kisses could fix the defect.

This isn't a grazed knee.

I keep hanging on to the belief that if I love him enough...

I squeezed him until he complained. If I squeeze hard enough, will I eradicate the poison from him, like pus from a spot?

I lean over and pull his sleeping body closer to me, wrapping him in my arms. In my head, I make promises. Deals with anyone who is listening. Please keep him safe.

23:49

Jake had pleaded with me tonight to let him go back to school after the weekend. He sensed my reluctance; *wise for his years,*

Mum always claimed *he's an old soul.* My mum's clichés comfort me like a weighted blanket, heavy and encompassing. They make my rational thoughts fight for space in my head. My ears ring with the strange, high-pitched tone of my mum's voice, which sounds as if it has a hint of helium in it. I picture her hair, forever set in tight ringlets that are outdated and grey: flashes of lightning in each curl. I use the smell of the bedsheets to draw on the memory of her Bold washing powder (the one I now buy in liquid form) which brings her back into my room with one whiff.

Her cruise, that I thought perfectly timed, now feels like an additional challenge for me to overcome. Tonight, no amount of remembered clichés or scented laundry will ease the worry wheedling its way through my head. Jake promised school would distract him. I couldn't tell him about the accidents I imagine happening there. How I need to shake my body to remove visions of him burning himself, being beaten up, or a tsunami wiping out the school when *SS Richard Montgomery* lets its load go. A reel of disaster films flicker through my head each time we are apart. The possibilities endlessly spiralling because of his prophecy. A helter-skelter ride I can't get off.

He asked to ring his dad again today. He cried because he hadn't rung him all week. Scared by the blood, Jake's fear reached a new level. I am in no doubt his intuition means something. How often do parents save children by following their gut instincts? All those near misses when adults joke about kids making it to adulthood. Sudden premonitions keeping them alive.

He knows. *An old soul.* He pretends to be okay, but even when distracted by his Xbox and life, he knows. The fear sits in the colour of his skin, in the dullness of his eyes, his deep-reaching concern for every tiny change in his body, his slim stature. Will he ever be a man? He must be in a constant state of high alert, the fight or flight response leaking chemicals into his bloodstream, poisoning his body. He doesn't understand it, but he knows.

He sobbed for an hour as I caressed his slight body, pulling it into mine, absorbing his tremors. They travelled along my fault lines. I knew a dose of my blue tablets would stop the earthquake breaking inside him. For me they remove the pain of long nights, and my fears along with them. I eased myself out of our hold and fetched him some water. My hand had hovered over the glass; the tablet squeezed between my fingertips. If I had cracked it open, I could have sprinkled the white powder into the water and he would have drank it without knowing.

'Mum, are you coming?' His plea stopped me. I paused in the bathroom, then pushed the tablet into my pocket instead.

He hadn't needed it. Five more minutes of cuddles and whispered clichés stolen from my mum encouraged him to drift off to the place in his head where he felt safe, despite his body lying there unprotected and vulnerable with sleep.

I hadn't drugged him, but he had slept. Knowing this does not help me find sleep.

01:23

His R2-D2 clock flashes its numbers onto the wall with a press of a button. I wriggle my arm out from under him. Balancing on an elbow, I admire the beautiful lines of his face where his jaw curves upwards to his cheek bone. Placing my hand on his chest, I feel his strong and steady breaths. Once, as a toddler he claimed his heart felt funny. He hadn't mentioned it for years but I now connect that unusual comment to my mum's irregular heart rhythm, undiagnosed until her mini-stroke, and something clicks. Had Jake known as he toddled and fell? Had he known that something inside him was defective back then?

He might look worried, a bit pale and thin, but not ill. Not like Matthew.

I cling to the rationality of that statement. I ignore the fact that in life things rarely make sense. I slither off the bed. At the door, I pause and watch him a little longer. The infinite blue numbers of his clock click over. 01:27.

I take the unopened blue tablet from my robe and collect three more. Tipping them into my mouth, I swig from the bathroom tap, ignoring the funny-tasting water as I swallow large gulps. A bubble of air sticks in my throat. Maybe this is what drowning feels like. Water going down with air and filling your lungs. I cough and wipe my lips on the flannel, smelling the toothpaste stains before I see them. I fling it into the wash basket and go back to my own, cold bed.

14 Days

My skin moves more easily than I would like as I slide a micellar water soaked cotton ball over my face. The deep circular motions are meant to 'invigorate blood flow and enliven the skin'. Instead the harsh bathroom light sucks away any progress I might be making. My skin looks worse than Jake's did when he surfaced at midday from a sweaty, over long sleep. Does his late morning mean he is lethargic? Is it another symptom? He had allowed me to mollycoddle him with pancakes, eaten under his duvet in front of the TV. I joined him, making him bend his knees so I could squeeze onto the end of our two-seater sofa. As a baby, he would lay on my lap, his head between my knees and his feet kicking my pillowy stomach. He is bigger and stronger now, yet him filling my sofa does nothing to address my worries about his health.

With my face washing routine finished, I am back on the landing. I pause at the top of the stairs, deciding what to do. Go to bed or go to Jake? Darkness swallows everything on the landing except my thoughts. Nothing on TV had managed to hold my attention and an attempt at a relaxing bath had made me feel worse with its obligation to feign relaxation whilst soaking under lavender-scented bubbles and aromatherapy oils. My bedroom offers little solace either. Its shades of lemon and grey, which I chose so it would offer a grown-up sanctuary for us, has started to resemble a prison cell. Paralysed by my indecision, I listen to the night. The sound of the boiler breaks out from the shadows, followed by the crunch of Malcolm on the road outside. Walking his dog again. A tap drips somewhere. A gull calls out.

Knock-knock.

I freeze. No one knocks on my door. Only my mum, when arriving uninvited. The Amazon delivery guy perhaps? I stay still. Did I order something?

Knock. Knock.

I think of Hugh's crowbar. Leaning over the banister, I look down the stairs at the partial shape visible through the glass panel. I wish I had a full wooden door with a peephole. I turn to check on Jake's door. Pulled to but accessible. The book I read for my A-Levels springs to mind, *In Cold Blood*. The one where Nancy Clutter was shot to death while tucked up in bed. All for the few pounds her father had in his safe.

Knock. Knock.

Burglars won't even find a few pounds in this house. I tip toe downstairs and through to the lounge, where, when I reach the far side of the room, I can pull the edge of the blind a fraction to reveal who is standing on my step. Malcolm steps back and looks up at the dark windows. Jake's window. He shakes his head as if he is talking to someone and telling them how strange his neighbours are with their house in darkness all day.

Hugh's SUV remains on the drive. Lights still flash around in his front room. A *Die Hard* marathon?

Malcolm reaches into the top pocket of his shirt and pulls out a small notepad and pen. He leans on my front door. The biro taps like Morse code on the glass panel. When his hirsute fingers appear through the letterbox, missing its guard after a vigorous delivery by the postie snapped it off, I recoil. A note flutters to the floor.

I keep watch from the lounge as he cuts across my drive and onto his own property. His gravel crunches again and his security light announces his return home. I dash to the hallway and pick up the note. I sit on the bottom step of the stairs and concentrate on breathing. I grip the folded paper. I hold it flat so I can see the words. The letters fade towards the end of the note. The angle of his pen on the door must have caused the ink to fail. A scribbled mark at the edge had brought the biro back to life.

Just checking you are o.k. Noticed your blinds were down all day again. Call if you need anything. Malcolm. No. 68. NWT.

Neighbourhood Watch Team.

I screw up the paper into a ball and go to the kitchen to throw it into the recycling, stuffing it under the bean can and the collapsed cereal box. The deeper it's buried, the less it will intrude into my thoughts.

On second thoughts, I pull it back out. I light it on the gas stove.

Flames lick at the paper. Black ash creeps towards my hand. Wisps drop into the sink. I let it burn the tops of my fingers before letting the remnants fall into the bowl of old washing up water. The scorched pancake pan is still soaking. With his interference extinguished, I turn on the tap and swill the remnants down the sink, pushing an escaped bean down the plughole with it rather than fishing it out. *Careful you don't block the sink with that food waste; I don't want to be taking out the u-bend to fish it out.* Without Dave, do I know how to take off the u-bend? I hope I haven't blocked it.

I turn my back to the sink and its gurgling drain. Leaning against the kitchen side, I follow the second hand around the clock. I pull off the letter stuck to the side of the broken microwave with a magnet and read it again. The doctor has requested a stool sample. We discussed this at our first appointment — possible bacteria from the takeaway or from the Norfolk seawater. They might be able to identify the cause of his issues. The blue flag on the beach is clearly no indicator of how safe it might be to swallow the North Sea. Tankers pass Sheppey on the way into the Thames Estuary so Norfolk is probably the same. Clear blood test results seemed to eliminate the need for a sample but now, with the reappearance of blood, the flash of red on the toilet paper, I am grateful the doctor is still considering further investigations. Jake will worry though. Another set of results for him to wait for. Can children develop stomach ulcers from worry? He gets them in his mouth already but I always have, so it didn't seem like a big deal. Could they be an underlying symptom, so benign I failed to notice? Has my incompetence as a parent meant something has gone undiagnosed? Will the diagnosis be too late to fix him? Will my ignorance about his health haunt me? I see myself at his graveside. Imagine his coffin, not quite adult-sized, but a gleaming ebony. Far more opulent than I can realistically afford. Crumbs of dark soil patter on the wood as they fall from my hands. The solemn words of the vicar. The pain on everyone's faces. His coffin being lowered into the earth. My broken voice pleading for forgiveness as I bury my son.

Phil's voice creeps into my head. *When your thoughts escalate, Vivian, when the rollercoaster starts to get out of control, grab a pen to slam on the brakes. Take action. Black on white. Ink on paper. Concrete and real. A list can help ease that rollercoaster ride to a pace where you can disembark safely.*

Write yourself to a stopping point and get off.

I grab my journal and write a plan of the things I can do:

- *Keep Jake home*
- *Keep a more detailed food diary for Jake*
- *Maintain the toilet diary with added detail*
- *Keep blinds closed*
- *Don't call Dave*
- *Don't answer the phone*
- *Keep Jake home*
- *Keep Jake home*
- *Keep Jake home.*

13 Days

21:00

'Go to your room.'

'Why, you gonna lock me up?'

'Now!'

My eyes don't leave Jake's until he moves up the stairs. For a moment I think he will disobey me, but his eyes drop and he turns away. His feet pound the floorboards and my grip tightens around my journal. He had screamed at me. Waved it in my face. Hurt by the words about his dad. I tried to explain that writing things down helps. *They're only words*. I avoided talking about my anxiety. He pleaded to go to school. To see his dad. He cried. Refused to eat so that I couldn't record it in his book. I cried.

His door slams shut.

I walk away and cross the kitchen. Turning the handle on the back door, I open it a fraction. I want to leave. To go outside and breathe in the sea air. Without Dave or my mum, I am trapped in my own home. I open the door wide, take my dad's cardigan off the chair, and walk to the boundary of the garden instead. Standing on the step, I look over the fence. I am as far away from Jake as it is possible to be without leaving my property. *Give him space,* my mum would advise. As if parenting me made her the oracle. The pull of him, deep inside me, like the remains of his umbilical cord clinging on, stop me. I attempt to scream into the night. Nothing escapes. My lungs won't let the pain go. Jake will hear me scream and he already thinks I'm crazy.

I sit on the step. I let my body droop. With my nose almost touching the fence, years of creosote permeating the wood seeps into my nostrils. Regardless of our preventative maintenance, rot set in last winter and now I can flake each plank with my fingers. Chips of wood and dust collect on the floor near the foot of the ladder. The smell of damp wood makes me long for the comfort of a log fire. My fingers create a hole through the fence and as it grows, I spy the nettles bordering the field beyond my house. I reach through and stroke the top of a green leaf, tempting it to sting me. It doesn't work. I pull my fingers back out the gap and bite at the peeling skin near my nails. The pain helps.

Is Jake chewing his fingernails? Or is he sleeping off his tantrum? Or attacking someone in one of his games?

I look behind me at the house. Thirteen days until his

birthday. Another bad omen? Our house stares back at me. It holds no answers: only empty windows and rotting frames. Not the family home I imagined when I fell pregnant at forty. I gaze at the stars and the moon. I will apologise to Jake and tell him that he is my stars and my moon. My world.

Knock. Knock.

I ignore the door. Probably Malcolm again.

'Hellooo?' Vocal chords rusty with age bellow over the fence. I can hear the rattling of the latch on the side gate but it's bolted on my side so whoever it is won't get in. I think about Jake upstairs in his room, as far away from me as he can be. I run into the house, taking two stairs at a time and fling open his bedroom door.

'Jake?' His bed covers are crumpled over an empty bed.

'Jake?' I shout louder. My neck jolting side to side as I scan upstairs. I fling open the bathroom door. Empty.

'Mum?' Jake's voice is faint.

'Hellooo? Anyone home?'

'Mum, answer the door!'

His voice drifts in from outside.

'Jake?' I race back to the garden gate, following the edge of the house with my hands for balance. I try to force the bolt, stiff with rust like the voice with Jake. Malcolm's voice. I try to keep my curses under my breath. 'Sorry. I'm trying to open it. It won't budge.' Jake is with Malcolm. I can't get to him. I groan as

I put all my weight behind the lock.

'Go to the front door, Mum.'

I rush back down the path. Stumbling over uneven paving slabs. Through the house. The hallway is dark. I yank the front door open, grab Jake by the collar of his coat and pull him into my arms. I look up at Malcolm. I look back down at Jake.

'Where've you been?' Tears well in his eyes.

'He's frightened he'll be in trouble. I told him that wouldn't be the case.'

I want to ask Malcolm not to speak for my son but I cannot form the words. I push Jake away from my body by the shoulders, inspecting him for harm. His rucksack hangs on Malcolm's back. I hold out my hand for him to return it to me and pull Jake closer to me as he approaches.

'I found him sat on the wall by the Co-op. With his rucksack and sleeping bag.'

'What the hel—' I stop myself, 'heck, Jake?'

'I thought I'd go to Dad's,' he whimpers and hides in the folds of his grandpa's cardigan. I gather my manners and offer my politest smile.

'Thank you...Malcolm. We'll be okay now.' I start to close the door. He leans in closer.

'You okay now, Jake?' Malcolm taps him on the shoulder and bends down to look him in the eye.

'Yeah.'

'Well, I'm next door kid, if you need me.'

'We're fine.' My tight voice snaps. 'Night.'

I shut the door. Malcolm shadows the glass for a moment longer. When his footsteps retreat, I squeeze Jake until he claims he can't breathe. We walk upstairs together. Both too afraid to speak.

01:11

Jake is asleep in my bed, taking up more than his fair share of space. I happily cling to the edge of the mattress, my arm resting on his hips. My nose is close enough to smell the sea on his skin. Watching him sleep is enough tonight.

12 Days

Jake home sick today.
10:26 Malcolm walks his dog.
12:31 No sign of Hugh or Leanne yet.

Recording the movements of the street has taken on new importance since Jake's attempt at running away. I need to be extra vigilant.

When Malcolm returned him, it confirmed for me that he must be scrutinising our every move. He'd waited for Jake to leave the house and then followed him to the shop. The dog walk was clearly a ruse. I have heard the term grooming before, but without the gifts, and the compliments, I had not seen this attention for what it was. Well, I recognise Malcolm's plan now alright. He'd saved Jake so Jake would trust him. With Jake's prophecy, I should have seen this coming.

I'm next door kid, if you need me.

So blatant. And in front of me too. I didn't want to scare Jake but I told him not to talk to our elderly neighbour without me. I tried to make Malcolm sound frail and vulnerable so that Jake wouldn't realise how much he should fear the predator living on our street. *He means well, but we must not take advantage of his kindness.* The lie tasted bitter on my tongue.

He asked me if I wanted to do some woodwork with him. It sounds fun.

No. Fear had made my voice squeak.

I tried to soften it. Pulled back my snappiness.

Leave him to his retirement, Jake. We're busy. You've got Scouts and...

I need to distract Jake, so he doesn't go to Malcolm looking for anything. I'll focus on the things he likes. I remember the rucksack, discarded under his dressing gown, in the corner of his room. We need time and space to get through the next twelve days. We need to be away from our phones. From interference. From everything.

The school keep chasing me. *We would like you to come in Mrs Farrington, for a chat about Jake.* When they rang today, I wanted to scream TIME. Time. You can't have my time with him. If this is it and I let him go to school, my time will be lost and I'll have fewer moments to hang my life on. You can't have my time. *I understand*, I said instead.

Will he be coming on the French school trip?

No.

Oh but you've paid the final balance. If it's about his treatment, it's perfectly manageable. We take children with far more serious conditions on trips abroad. Our staff are fully trained. I wanted to say, you wouldn't take them if you knew something terrible would happen. Not if you knew they might die. You wouldn't take them then, would you? I wanted to scream down the phone. My knuckles whitened as I gripped the receiver. I listened to the sound of the phone line for a moment. Composed myself as an entire ocean swooshed down the cable to me.

I'd rather he stayed home. It doesn't matter about the money. Not that I won't accept a refund if they offer me one.

I'm afraid the insurance won't cover a refund if it's your decision not to let him travel. He'd need a doctor's certificate for that. The secretary seemed to read my mind. *So we'll see him tomorrow then. With you. Before registration for our chat.* I felt as lost now as I had when I hung up.

I line up Jake's uniform on the hanger, straightening the shoulders and collar. I place it over the towel rail so it'll be warm in the morning. His polished shoes sit near the front door. I do the final job and wipe marks from his coat with a wet wipe. Picking a spot of mud from the sleeve with my nail. Everything is ready apart from me.

Jake has been looking forward to the school trip to France for months. In fact, since we looked around the school in the autumn term of Year 6 and the head teacher had shown his new class a slide show of the things they could expect from their new 'outstanding school'. Smiling children stuffed crepes into their open mouths, lemony syrup dripping down their chins. French flags flew off the coast of Arromanche and the long flat beaches, which looked remarkably like those on Sheppey, flicked across the screen. I thought of *SS Richard Montgomery* and the history we have on the island. Why do they need to go to France?

I play out our conversation in my head: how I will break the news that he won't be going in the Eurotunnel. I must tell him he can stop practising how to ask for milk in his tea and tomato ketchup for his French fries. I smile as I remember explaining they are just frites in France, *you can drop the French*. How many other things will I not have to explain to him if he isn't going? He talked about wanting croissants the size of his head. Chocolate éclairs even larger. Every time I play the conversation in my head, Jake ends up in tears. I end up the bad guy. And what if he gets angry again?

You gonna lock me up?

His words were coated in hatred. Not since he left behind

the terrible twos, which if I am honest lasted until he reached four, had he spoken to me so harshly. I dismiss those difficult times. There is no room in my head for scolding words and disappointed faces. I need twelve years of perfect memories to sustain me.

02:12

Keep Jake safe.

I trace the words with my fingers. He cannot go to France. The lie I will tell starts to form at the edges of my mind. I can be the good guy. Console him. On the morning of the trip, I will fake a call from the teacher. The trip is cancelled due to...an outbreak of flu in the hotel. No. There are other hotels. They would arrange a substitute. An outbreak of flu in the school staff. Due to staff shortages, those supposed to go on the trip can stay home and do their own World War II research on the island. We will visit the pillbox at Warden Point, *SS Richard Montgomery* (from the safety of the beach) and I can create a whole schedule for our own school trip. He'll be disappointed but it'll give us time and space. He'll be safe.

His rucksack will be waiting for him, packed and ready, and I'll suggest we go camping. Wild camping. So he'll still get away. Like the trips he took with Dave. A getaway to ease the disappointment. I'll let him soak up the thought of staying at home first and then surprise him, like one of those laid-back mums who are spontaneous and never say no to anything, even chocolate for breakfast or ice creams before dinner. *No, you don't have to put your coat on. No, you don't have to wear shoes outside. Shoes? Shoes are for ninnies. Get hot aches. Forget about cleaning your teeth. Live a little, Jake.*

I place my notebook down and notice that Hugh's SUV is no longer facing the house. Someone must have reversed it up against the front door. The boot sits wide open. The light inside illuminates the cabin. Bulging black bin liners fill the doorway of the renovated bungalow. Hugh lugs each one to the boot and chucks them in. He presses the remote and it closes over the bin bags with a shush and clunk. Blue lights flash in his lounge window like before. He closes the front door.

I make a note of his activity next to my list of things I will do with Jake instead of letting him go to France. Another list below details everything I might need for an impromptu camp-out. Hugh's activities look banal as I record them but I do it just in case. In case of what? I add there is still no sign of Leanne. Could Leanne be in those bin bags? Would anyone leave their wife in their boot and go back to the TV? To *Die Hard*?

I sit forward on my bed to look over at Malcolm's house. Why would he watch me and Jake, and not Hugh? An unhealthy interest in boys, that's why. The street begins to feel smaller; my windows larger. I draw the blinds.

Nowt queer as folk, my mum's response to anything she can't easily explain springs to mind. It doesn't help me now.

I go to the bathroom cabinet. My supply of sleeping tablets, prescribed for occasional use, is running low. Getting it re-filled so soon might be difficult with the lady on reception guarding the doctors' time. How often have I been taking them recently? More than fortnightly, I know that much. I place two in my hand. It should be enough to get me through until dawn.

11 Days

'Mum! Mum!'

I can hear his voice but the words sound muddy and wet in my ears.

'Mu-umm!' Something heavy weighs me down and my stiff body won't respond to his call. As I peel off my covers, cold air hits my damp skin. The door bangs open, crashing into the plaster wall. Dave never did fit the bloody door stop. The hole must be even bigger now. 'Mum?'

'Jake? What time is it?' My voice sounds gravelly.

'16:16.' He reads the digital display on his phone. 'Mum, why are you in bed? The house is all dark. Have you been in bed since you dropped me off at school?' His words hit me like bullets. I roll over and try to push myself up. I shudder as my body adjusts to being awake. I spy my pill bottle next to my lamp. The lid sits next to it. I shift in bed to block it from Jake's view. I vaguely recall the thick fog we walked through to school.

The attendance officer's interrogation of my parenting skills. The humiliating offers of support. *Shall I ring his dad and call him in for a chat too?*

'Mum? Did you? Jake's voice has a new quality. A high pitched accusatory tone I've never heard from him before.

'No...I'm fine.' The words stick in my throat and lack the authority I intended to convey.

'But...'

'Shhh, Jake.'

'Shall I open the blind?' He starts to move towards the window but keeps his eyes on me.

'No, Jake.'

'Shall—'

'Just go watch TV. I'll be down in a minute.' Jake backs out of the room, closing the door behind him so quietly that I barely hear the click of the latch over my own heavy breathing.

23:12

I stir in bed and try to remember what day it is. I need to reduce my sleeping tablets as I'm definitely getting confused. I get up and go to Jake's bedroom. He must have put himself to bed. A smattering of crumbs form a trail across his desk.

'Jake, did you eat at your computer?'

He doesn't reply. His phone is next to his pillow. Dead. I put it on charge and go back to my room.

The fusty smell of sweaty sheets clogs my nostrils. I pull at the blind; its mechanism screeching into the dark room. Under the security light, Malcolm waits with his dog. He is staring up at my bedroom window.

I drop the blind's pulley. It clatters against the glass and I step back.

Standing at the corner of the blind, I peer out. He's disappeared. The security light has extinguished, but the waning moon highlights the small particles of quartz in the paving slabs that run in parallel lines down to the house. For a moment the beauty of each sparkle stops my mind whirring. Then I spot weeds running over the middle section. Dandelion fairies bash each other in the breeze. I must pick one tomorrow so Jake can make a wish. And one for me, to plead with fate to save him.

I slump onto the edge of the mattress. How can I stop Malcolm staring at our house?

Picking up my phone, I consider Googling restraining orders but the mention of *SS Richard Montgomery* on my newsfeed makes me scroll down. It has made the headlines again after a near miss with a tanker coming into the Thames, its navigation tools interrupted by thick fog. A last-minute redirection avoided a catastrophic collision. Experts remind the local news crew that if the sunken armoury explodes, the gas cylinders on the

Isle of Grain will create tidal waves sufficient to reach London. As usual there is no mention of the fact that such waves will probably submerge the entire of Sheppey.

A Twitter notification pops up in front of me. You might be interested in *Last Photos Before People Died*. The title-picture features the *Fast and Furious* star in a brooding pose, leaning against his car hours before his death, like James Dean. Cinematic icons forever. I can't remember his name. Jake would know it. I click on the link and expect to see celebrity after celebrity *cut down in their prime*. The 27 Club. I hear my mum's voice and look over my shoulder — an empty room looks back at me. I turn to the window again — the street is empty too. On my phone Heath Ledger stares through me. He made the list but I soon realise these photos are mainly normal people like me and Jake. Selfies taken from the edge of clifftops moments before the victims fell. Family snaps at parties before fatal car crashes on the way home. Smiling faces in a stadium full of music fans, the air bursting with music moments before a mad man shot into the crowd, or a street full of pedestrians going about their day before a suicide bomber flicked a switch. A photo of a fireman at a baseball game with his son the day before 9/11.

I reach image thirty-six before I shut down the link, unable to face any more dead strangers. Opening the photo app on my phone, I find the last picture I took of Jake, of him hanging from the pull-up bar in the kitchen. His arms taut; his legs dangling. Dave's pull-up bar, which friends and family had to duck under or risk a concussion. He'd taken it with him when he left. Had I taken no photos since? Not one. Not even in Norfolk? There must be photos on Jake's phone. His selfie prowess always surpasses mine. That holiday without Dave had taken guts and bravery to book. Three months of Jake changing and growing, and I have no evidence of these precious moments. All now lost to time. Time I don't have.

I pad across the landing and turn on the flash, aiming the focus square over Jake's head. I click and take a burst of photos of him sleeping. I'll take more tomorrow.

I go further back on my camera roll and scroll through hundreds of old snaps. Jake filthy in the woods last autumn, clean and in his pyjamas before bed, smiling last Christmas between a small mountain of presents, gurning last Easter with his face squeezed between two chocolate eggs, his last birthday with his legs astride his new BMX and his feet tucked into a new pair of trainers, the laces luminous white. Very few of me or Dave, even less of us all together. There's one selfie of all three of us from our visit to Pizza Express when we used the vouchers Dave's folks had bought us for Christmas. They haven't been in touch since he left either but then that isn't surprising as they rarely got in touch before.

My phone flashes low battery status. 23:59.

I wiggle the cable into the charging port until it vibrates. I close my eyes. The last photos of those people, moments before their deaths, project onto the back of my eyelids.

I click open the bottle on my bedside table and take two tablets with my glass of water from yesterday, ignoring the dust particles settled on the surface from the day before. I close my eyes and wait for the film of dead faces to stop.

10 Days

23:12

The grain of the wood from the dining table presses into my forehead. I push harder, wood against bone. As I increase the pressure, I listen to the noises of the house. The usual creaks and groans but nothing that could be Jake. No sounds of *Fortnite*, or *Plants Vs Aliens*, or *Rocket League* penetrate the room. Where is he? I cast my mind back to this morning. I had woken with tremors rippling down my arms. My mind swelled with the heaviness of the omen I'd dreamt about. It wasn't safe for Jake to leave the house. I begged him to stay home. My gut insisted with him.

His protests are fresh in my mind. It must have been today.

I think I should go in, Mum. It's PE and DT again. I feel okay. My test results are clear. And I've already missed one experiment in science.

I had pleaded with him, my words contorted by the shape of my mouth. *I need you to stay home today, Jake.* Words stuck to my gums.

Mum, you're talking funny...are you okay?

Yeah, just tired sweetheart.

Had he stayed home today? Or was that yesterday? The extra tablets I had taken when I stirred in the early hours must have been making my words slur. The alarm broke through my morning fog but it didn't lift me out from under the weight of it. Jake had finally agreed to stay home when I promised he could play Xbox all day. It was definitely this morning.

He had smiled. A cheeky look of surprised satisfaction. He'd expected a no. Or a negotiation at least. I'd thought of sand trickling through a timer and pondered how many grains he had left. I couldn't argue with my head so full of water. *Shut the door on the way out, would you.*

But then his Xbox noise had driven me mad. Yes, definitely today. I screamed at him to turn it down or turn it off. All the battle noises hammered my head. Where is he now? The noise has gone.

I leave the dining table to find him. The kitchen's empty. I sweep his crusts from the breadboard, stale and much larger than if I'd sliced them off. Dried cheese curls out at the edge of the crusts. He must have eaten. The boundaries of night and day blur around me.

Where is he? In bed? I refocus. My hands are holding the bin lid. What am I doing? Water will help clear my head. I'm probably dehydrated. My sleeping tablets always make it worse. I refill my glass.

00:11

I take small sips. I cannot stand the tap water from the bathroom sink. *It's the same water Viv,* but despite Dave's reassurances I know it's different somehow and not good for me. I fill Jake a glass to take up to his room. He must be in bed. The doctor said he must drink more fluids too and although there is a crisp packet and the dried peel from a satsuma and the box from the Jaffa Cakes wedged into the recycling, I can't see an empty glass anywhere.

00:23

Jake is in bed, one leg hanging over the edge. His breathing rhythmic. I put the glasses of water down and place my hand over his ribs. His diaphragm enlarges; swelling and deflating under my palms. I mirror his breathing, slowing my own breaths by using him as a metronome. He looks healthy, a layer of puppy fat is beginning to develop around his middle. Twelve Jaffa Cakes inside his stomach. Digesting. Travelling their way through his gut, leaving their calories behind.

My hands stay still. His eyes move under their lids and I

remember he often slept with his eyes slightly open as a baby in his Moses basket. We joked we had birthed the devil child. I tried to close his eyelids, like they do on dead bodies in films, but they always popped back open, as if on springs. As if he didn't want to miss a moment of life. Had he known as a baby how short his life would be?

Jake coughs and I lift my hand as he rolls over. I rub his back for a second and he pulls away, shuffling from underneath my touch towards the wall. I take my glass from his desk and stand back, waiting for his breathing to settle into a new rhythm. Backing away, one step at a time, I keep my eyes on him until I'm on the landing. I hesitate. What should I do now?

I imagine Jake's bed empty; his room redundant. I have to stop this continuous cycle of catastrophising going on in my head.

My brain needs to stop. I head for the bathroom. My tablets are still on the edge of the sink. Top already off. I tip two tablets into my mouth. Staying awake in my head tonight won't work. There are too many possible scenarios that all end with me losing Jake.

9 Days

I shake my head side-to-side, then up and down, anything to
dislodge the endless cycle repeating the day's conversations,
letting them worm their way through my mind. I can't shut out
Dave's exasperated tone, accusing me of driving a wedge
between him and Jake, as if he hadn't done that by himself
when he left without saying goodbye.

I breathe out, trying to release the tightness of the guilt
gripping my insides by using the short sharp exhalations we
were taught in yoga. Dragon breathing to detoxify and relax.
The fire burns on inside me as another repetition of Dave's
words resounds in my head.

*You gave the school an incorrect number for me, Viv. What if
there'd been a real emergency and not just a text message
bouncing back? What if they couldn't get hold of you?*

What if? What if? What if? Dave has no idea how these two
tiny words torment me. The echo of his what ifs making my

catastrophising worse. I wanted to say he had no right to condemn my parenting decisions. I'm the one who is present. They will be able to get through to me Dave, I wanted to say. I'm alert all the time, awaiting the emergency. I check my phone every fifteen minutes without fail; have had to train myself to not check it more often because the battery life can't sustain such constant use, and thanks to your departure I can't afford to upgrade it. I roll my shoulders and crick my neck. Dave can piss off. As can the school secretary who told him his phone number didn't work when he rang to let them know of his change of address. She somehow remembered, and made sure to tell him when he rang, that I had changed his number. I remember her judgemental tone. The tone she uses to query Jake's absences. She probably spent her morning break stood at the water machine gossiping about me. *You know Jake F? The one with the floppy blonde fringe and freckles? That TA's son.*

Yeah. His mum gave us an incorrect number for his dad. Her ex? Yeah. Can you believe it? Poor kid. No wonder she is still off work. Psycho bitch. She's lost it.

Or worse, a pitiful tone. *Poor woman. Fallen apart since he left. He ran off with a colleague apparently. Left the island behind too. Who can blame him, eh?*

I shake out every limb. Trying to discard the image of the school staff, my colleagues, gossiping about me. I try to release my stiff muscles at the same time. Re-focussing on Malcolm's driveway, I let the condensation from my breath gather on the glass and shake my head this time. 'Wake up, Vivian. Be present.'

Mum! Mum! Mummm! He'd had to call me three times this morning before he gave up and came to find me. I was staring into the full coffee pot. Steam gathering on my glasses. He teased me, *you auditioning for the next season of The Walking Dead?* He'd been shouting because he needed more toilet paper in the upstairs bathroom.

Mum! Mumm! Mummmm! I glance over my right shoulder, then my left, disorientated by his voice. There is no one there. His voice is in my head. A memory. How come I couldn't hear him this morning and now his words reverberate in my ears until I want nothing more than to rip my head from my shoulders?

I wipe the glass door panel with my dressing gown sleeve. Goose-bumps gather on my arms as the damp fluff touches my skin.

Malcolm left to walk the dog fifteen minutes ago. He paused at the end of my drive and scanned each window. The dog pulled on his lead making Malcolm move but not before he had stroked his chin several times. He'd done the same on my doorstep earlier. Pulling the concerned neighbour face.

Just wondered if you and Jake were okay?

Yes.

*Oh, it's just that I'd noticed he's not been at school much
again. Unwell is he?*

Has been.

And you? You're okay?

I could see his discomfort but I had no intention of filling in
the awkward silences. *I'm good. You?* I thought deflecting the
questions back to him might get rid of him but he started
talking about his bird-watching. The finches visiting my
sycamore. His disappointment at the speed his sapling grew.
How mighty and unruly my specimen now was. He kept
peering past me into the hallway so I used my bare foot to push
the door closed, a little at a time. To block his view of the house,
I raised my arms. The bat wings of my dressing gown blocking
the gaps.

*Just wondered if Jake would like to do some woodwork with
me? Build a bird box, maybe?* I stared at his beard: grey and
wiry. His eyes set back in his head looked like his Jack Russell's,
dark and small, like black pearls. His hands, the soft, puffy flesh
of the old. *Jake home, is he?*

Yes. But he's busy. Anything else I can get you, Malcolm?

No. No. He seemed to be giving up and stepping back so I
relaxed a little. Let my guard down. He tripped, or seemed to,
stumbled forward into the door, pushing it out of my hands
and wide open. I had no choice but to step back otherwise he
would have fallen on me. *Sorry,* he claimed. But his eyes darted

up the stairs, along the hallway and into the kitchen. *Sorry*. He said it again. Louder. Trying to attract someone's attention.

I pushed him upright and closed the door on his feet until he had to extricate himself from my property to avoid injury.

No problem. The false nonchalance remains in my voice, hours later. It lingers with me in the hallway while I wait to see if he'll watch us or if he'll leave us alone. It's Jake he wants, not me. The stranger danger videos we watched at school during assemblies had weird characters asking inappropriate questions. *Do you want to come to my house to see my puppies? Do you want to come to my house to build a bird box?* Surely a predator would not hunt so close to home? But most victims know their attackers, don't they?

Malcolm's outside light bursts into life as his dog, on an extended lead, wanders onto his own property. He sniffs the late-flowering hydrangea in Malcolm's border and gives it a last swish of urine before Malcolm appears from the road as if it is he who has been walked. The lead retracts into its case whipping and curling in on itself. Malcolm stares in my direction. I freeze. Holding my breath to avoid the moisture gathering on the obscured glass. Malcolm opens his front door and shoos the dog in but not before one last look at Jake's bedroom window.

The drive and road are silent. I move my stake-out upstairs to the landing. Malcolm's house, from this angle, shows no signs of life so I risk retiring to my bedroom, as fatigue is making my eyes heavy and my muscles ache. After being folded by the glass door, my tendons and ligaments are frozen into position, reluctant to release their pose. I straighten my body out under the duvet, stretching to each corner of the bed. When I close my eyes, instead of sleep, I see Malcolm's black pearl eyes bore into Jake. I open them again, sit up and turn on the bedside lamp. I open *The Bell Jar* and read a page or two but I can't remember how the main character ended up at the magazine or what her name is. I close the book.

You changed my number, Viv. Why would you do that? Dave's voice starts again.

I cover my ears and scrunch my eyes closed. I wriggle under the covers, pulling every limb into my chest until I resemble an unborn child.

'Malcolm's watching. Dave's watching. Everyone is watching. Glaring. Judging.'

Someone is muttering in my room. I open my eyes. No one is there.

8 Days

With my knees wrapped up in my arms, I sway side-to-side, unable to settle in my Sherlock chair. Coffee beans coursing through my bloodstream make me jittery. I regret the three flat whites I drank today. I bought a take-away first, before my final group counselling session with Phil. I downed the other two sat in the café window, trying to distract myself from the fact I wasn't fixed. The sessions hadn't helped. I thought the nine shots would keep me alert and ready if Dave showed up unannounced to try and take Jake away. He'd practically accused me of abuse. They now careen through me, doing a caffeine somersault performance. Dave's sudden parental interest might be a sham but his charade probably impressed the school secretary. After all, she showed no female solidarity to me. *You can't trust other women.* Even though we are living through the third, or is it the fourth, wave of feminism, my mum still says that. I didn't understand it. Not until Dave left.

I check the landline is still unplugged. The connection located in the hallway sits next to the front door. A door that appears suddenly weak. So old that anyone could force the frame and gain entry to our home. I move the dining chairs and stack them in front of it.

> *21:56 White Astra parked outside number 16.*
> *22.01 Malcolm's lounge light out. Conservatory still on.*
> *No sign of Hugh or Leanne.*
> *22.14 Pick-up spins around at the T-junction.*

I record each passing car, no detail too small. Since Jake went to bed at nine, six vehicles have travelled down our road. All belonging to residents of the street if you count the people whose houses sit on the corner and use the road as a turning point. No visitors in the last forty-five minutes, other than the local cats. No sign of Smudge though.

I stretch out, brave enough to walk in front of the window now Malcolm has turned out his lights. I check; they're still out. If Dave turns up, he'll find my doors locked and barricaded, the phone line dead. I star jump to release the energy building up in my muscles. I need to discharge the caffeine. I flit across the room, unable to focus on anything for long but I am alert and ready.

02:55

There is movement outside; I dive back to my pad and pencil. Tripping over the metal door threshold, I graze my knee on the carpet. I brush myself off and record the activity.

> *Possible sighting of Leanne. Velux light in hall on.*
> *Extinguished 02:56. No visual on the victim.*

Hugh strolls past the downstairs window on his phone, scrolling through the screen.

03:01

I spin on my tiptoes and lose my balance, smashing my temple on the edge of my wardrobe.

'Fuck.'

I rub sweat from my brow as I try to subvert the pain in my head by applying pressure to the point of impact.

Where am I? I place my hand on the bed, run my fingers over my throw. The soft wool, a stale smell, a map. I am in my bedroom.

03:07

I read my notes but the words wobble. My heart races faster

than usual. The drum beat in my chest pounds, resonating in my ears and my feet and my fingers. I drop the notepad. Using the wall as a crutch, I guide my hand to take myself to the middle of the bed. I lay back and look at the ceiling. It spins. I open my eyes. The sharp pain in my temple starts to fade to a dull ache. I close my eyes again and try to ignore the pounding in my chest.

7 Days

21:14

Malcolm stands on Hugh's doorstep; the waxing moon hanging above him. His dog pulls on his leash as he urinates on Hugh and Leanne's grey topiary pots. The trees are already losing their clipped shape. Hugh leans one arm on the doorframe. I crane my neck to get a better look at him. He looks disinterested. I crack the window open a fraction, putting pressure on the hinge with my fingertips to soften any creaks. Malcolm turns. I stand back from the glass. He points towards my house and into the shadows. 'See.' He hisses through his teeth like a ventriloquist.

I drop to the floor, leaning my back against the cold radiator under the window. I strain to catch the next few words on the wind before the waves and the traffic whisk them away.

'Worried...the boy seems...at home...don't know...dad... missing...not surprised...Dave's number.'

The last words go up in pitch like a question. I grip the

windowsill and pull myself up into a crouch and view them out the bottom of the pane. Hugh doesn't appear to be saying anything and Leanne has not joined them at the door. I still haven't seen her. That's what Malcolm should be worried about.

'I...keep out...nosey neighbours...no idea mate.'

Clunk.

Hugh's composite, fake-wood door closes on Malcolm. I dip my head lower but keep my eyes on him. He stares at their black door as he walks away, shaking his head at the dog before stopping to let it piss up the plant pots properly. Tugging it along the drive, he crosses to his own property, but as he walks his eyes move to our house. He mutters to himself. 'Don't know them mate. Didn't even know she had a son. Young neighbours. Bloody useless.'

'Mum, what are you doing?' I think fast, swipe the flat of my hand across the pile of the carpet.

'I've lost an earring, Jake. Give us a hand will you.' As he drops to his knees, I slip a dangly earring from my lobe and hide it in the palm of my hand. I keep the pretence going for a few more seconds. He'd already questioned why the dining chairs were piled up against the front door this morning. Did he believe my lie about cleaning the carpet?

'Oh, here it is.' I wave it in front of him. 'It's one of the feather ones you bought me for Mother's Day.' Jake smiles and heads back to his room. 'Night then. Lights off at nine-thirty, yeah?'

'Laters.'

'Lights off at nine-thirty, yeah?'

'Yeah.'

I slump against the radiator, flinching as the cold metal catches my bare skin.

Will Malcolm try to contact Dave? He should be trying to find Leanne. Why would Dave be able to fix things for me? Incredulous, I start to get myself ready for bed, reminding myself that winding down, following a bedtime routine can improve the chance of sleep.

My new moisturiser from Amazon smells like fresh meadows as promised but feels like clay as I spread it on my face. I hope it will fill the lines sleep deprivation keeps leaving behind.

22:16

I flip my novel over and re-read the blurb. It doesn't clarify what I have read. Phil once suggested we use our extra time awake productively, finding purpose in order to abate the anger caused by being awake. I would rather sleep.

A few weeks ago, I found an old magazine in the lounge that listed 100 books you should read before you die. Hence *The Bell*

Jar. I sympathise with Esther and Sylvia but my exhaustion, though not sufficient to push me over the precipice of sleep, prevents me from focusing on any more than a paragraph at a time. I close the paperback and think I might need to find something trashier – perhaps not on the top 100 list. My eyes are begging to close so I let them go.

Jake stands in front of me, toddling on his fat wobbly legs. His white blonde fringe, curled at the tips, poking him in the eye. *Come to Mumma*, I call. The toddler gazes at me with adoring eyes and as he reaches out to me, he loses his balance. Between us a black hole opens to reveal an abyss so wide and deep he cannot avoid falling into it. His dungareed body disappears into the darkness. No screams emerge from the deep space. A swoosh of air passes between his sprawling arms and legs.

I jerk awake.

My fingertips clamp the duvet. I'm unsure if I screamed in my head or out loud. I can taste the noise on my tongue. I swing my legs down to the floor, checking for solid ground. I rush to Jake's room to check he's okay.

His bedside light is out. His earphones are in. I expect to see some grunge band that he's started listening to on the screen but pumping through his earphones are stories. Another Baddiel. Not the C S Lewis and J R R Tolkien I recommended. If I had screamed, he wouldn't have heard.

Searching on Facebook for Leanne is proving more difficult
than I expected. There are 117 Leannes on Sheppey alone.
Despite the things I know about my neighbour — her unhappy
marriage and unsuccessful IVF treatments — I have no idea of
her surname, maiden or married. Next time Malcolm knocks
on my door, I should tell him to look for Leanne. What could he
do though? Follow Hugh? Steal their mail? Spy on them too?

None of the Leanne profile pictures offer any clues. The
photos are too small to try and identify Leanne's delicate
features. I can dismiss those with dogs filling the circular space
though so my search results reduce to fifty-eight.

Some couples are sporting grey hair and a few have rainbow
flags promoting LGBTQ+ so I dismiss those ones too. Twenty-
one.

I haven't seen Leanne since the day after the crow bar
incident. She must have let Hugh in. When I checked the
morning after, his car had been on the drive, its door closed
and the headlights off. Since that night, Hugh has come and
gone but not with Leanne. Not even a sighting of her upstairs.
No lights under the VELUX. She must have gone. Or Hugh
makes it seem like she's gone. I think of the bin liners in his
boot.

In bold letters the words 'potentially dangerous and violent' flicker onto my phone screen. A Facebook notification alerting me that a convict has escaped from a Sheppey prison. I click on the link.

Ewan Horton, 37, who was jailed for armed robbery, went missing from HMP Standford Hill on the Isle of Sheppey earlier this evening. It is believed he travelled towards London and the public are urged not to approach him. Horton is about 5ft 9in and slim, with dark hair, blue eyes and a three-inch scar on his right cheek. He also has a tattoo with the words "Mum and Dad" on his right wrist and a tattoo with the word "Lily" on his left shoulder. Detective Lawrence, from Kent Police, said: "Horton is viewed as potentially dangerous and violent and I would urge members of the public to not approach him directly, but to immediately call the police." Horton is said to have links to Essex, Suffolk, London and Birmingham.

The convict must be searching the coastline for a way to cross to the mainland. He'll be on the other side of the island to me. Sea fog might have aided his escape already. Hopefully. I get up and look out into the street. Malcolm's outside with the dog again. Maybe the convict will get him. He pauses at my driveway for longer than he does at any other house on the street, except for Hugh's where Malcolm now lets his dog's leash fully extend so it can cock its leg up every topiary pot.

I need to pee too.

After washing my hands, I dab lavender oil on my wrists

(Amazon suggested it might help when I last purchased some sleepy tea) and grab the old eye mask from my travel wash bag. Maybe a total black out will block the faces of escaped convicts, spying neighbours and Hugh wielding his crowbar from my mind.

I settle into bed and adjust the straps of the mask. As soon as all the gaps of light are extinguished, I see Jake's dungarees disappearing down the black hole again.

I rip off the mask, snapping the elastic. I throw it across the room.

I listen at the wall for Jake's deep breathing and the sound of water trickling through his fish tank pump, listening for any sounds of life.

6 Days

18:01

Malcolm's been watching us all day. His binoculars were directed towards our blinds. Well, until he saw me returning his gaze, then he had the decency to swing them towards the sycamore. I try to move surreptitiously from one window to the next, but with my heavy limbs I am probably about as stealthy as Smudge: a cat who can only catch injured prey.

He has a notepad on the coffee table next to him and what looks like a cup of tea. The steam rises in his conservatory. It must be chilly in there.

Does he record his sightings of us? Does he have notes like mine? Similar to his RSPB survey but instead of tracking wildlife he's tracking the movements of the Farringtons. Next to the notebook sits Malcolm's cordless phone. Who is he planning to ring? Dave? School? Social services? The police?

All of them will think they know what is best for Jake but they don't know about his prophecy. I hear my mum, *stuck between a rock and a hard place, you are.*

If I tell anyone that I think Jake is going to die before his birthday, they will certify me insane. Lock me up under the Mental Health Act. They will think that I'll be the one putting him in danger. Particularly if they find out I'm lying to him about his school trip. His teachers are not sick. All of them are in France, without him. This morning he sulked for the first few hours but once he settled into the day he seemed to resign himself to my plan to do things here instead. No one will understand I did it to keep him safe, to change the course of fate.

I'll not allow him to be taken from me or this world before he even hits puberty.

I want those awkward conversations about girls, wet dreams and consent. He can like boys if he wants to. I want to clear up his vomit after a night partying on the beach, necking cider and alcohol the colour of toxic rainbows. I want to feed him bacon sandwiches and nurse his hangovers. To help him find a job or pick a college course. To help him find a route off the island, if that's what he wants.

Malcolm puts down his pen and his hand drifts to his waistband. Can he see me watching? I step back a little more in case the blinds don't give me the coverage I suppose they do. No, he's not looking at me. The light glints from his lenses at an angle that suggests Jake's room is his target. His hand reaches deeper inside his elasticated trousers. He repositions himself. I pull away from the window. My stomach turns. Saliva gathers in my mouth.

We need to leave. Now. Taking the car will draw too much attention. It'll be traceable. I recall Dave's fishing trips and his portable two-man tent. Jake willingly went with him while I stayed home. I can do this. I can be the fun parent who says yes to everything, even wild camping in early October. 'Jake?' I call out to him from my room.

'Yeah.'

'Do you fancy going camping?'

'Next weekend?'

'No, now.'

'Now?'

'Yeah. You'll still get the trip you were promised. But here rather than France.'

'Where?'

'Cliffside Farm. No one will be up there. It's out of season.'

'Really?'

'Yeah. Just this once. You know me and camping don't always go together.'

Jake pokes his head around the door. 'Hello and what have you done to my Mum?'

'Funny.'

'I'm not complaining.'

'Good. Go fill up your rucksack, get the tent out the shed and I will pop to Iceland for some supplies.'

19:57

'You ready, Jake?'

I lift the rucksack, now bulging with food, onto my back. The tent is strapped to it with bungee cords. I checked Malcolm's stakeout position in the conservatory. He's still there. He has a biscuit barrel on his knee and another cup of tea steaming next to him. His dog stands at his side. Tongue out. Waiting on the off chance of catching a crumb or two.

'Yep.'

Rushed but fairly certain we have everything — we must have with this weight — we leave the house. I pull the Yale closed, careful not to slam it. Hugh and Leanne's house looks empty across the road.

I take Jake's hand and pull him across the unadopted road, dodging potholes as we make for Eastend via the bridle ways. I look behind me, to both sides of the street and then all around. My head spinning like an anxious barn owl.

'You okay, Mum?'

'U-huh.'

'You look like you're freaking out.'

'No. No. Just thinking I hope we haven't forgotten anything.'

Once we are off the street, I force a smile on my face and try to relax. I left the lights on in the kitchen and hallway, and the bathroom window ajar so Malcolm will think we're home.

As we wind our way along the path to Eastend Farm, we pass alongside the farm-house and reach the 'Caution Cliff Erosion' signs advising us not to proceed. None of the locals take any notice; we're all well aware of the dangers of walking too close to the edge. I take no risks though and ensure Jake is on the inland side and keep as far away as possible from the edge as darkness sets in.

The walk drags on and my bag makes my shoulders ache. It's further than I remember to Cliffside and I'd forgotten the stretch along the main road without any footpaths. Stopping for each passing car slows our journey. We squint into the headlights and I hold my breath as exhaust fumes cover us. As we approach the caravan park, we carry on along a private road, passing the cliff path we'll use tomorrow to reach the shingle beach, and turn onto the public road, Fourth Avenue. A few hundred yards further on and we pass a caravan graveyard. Window frames and wooden units rotting alongside broken doors and empty gas bottles. I re-adjust my rucksack to relieve the ache in my shoulders as we reach the boundary of the next field. 'Nearly there.'

'Good. Do you want me to carry that?'

I look at his small frame. 'Next time, when you're bigger.' I try to keep the worry off my face. What if there isn't a next time?

We cross a stile into one of the fields that borders the edge of the island. We can see the top rooms of Cliffside Farm lit up in the distance. 'We'll camp this side of the pond.' I point to a large flat area as far from the paddock and farm as possible. No one will even know we're here.

21:07

'Give it here, Mum. You flick it, like this.' With the turn of Jake's wrist the dome of the two-man tent pops to life.

'It's pretty flimsy... and small.'

'You don't need much to keep you warm if the space is small. Dad always said it wouldn't withstand a rainstorm though.' We both look up at the clear sky and see the stars are brighter now we're away from the light pollution of the town. 'No clouds means no rain, right?' The wind nearly whips the canvas from Jake's hands. 'Help me peg it down, Mum.'

Together we grapple our portable bedroom from the wind. We set up the stove and kettle and lay out our sleeping mats and bags in two neat rows. Perfect. Jake clambers in and lies down on his back, flicking through something on his phone. 'WhatsApp?'

'Nah. YouTube.'

'Oh. I was hoping that we could have a break from all that for a few days.'

'A few days...mmm okay.' He carries on scrolling.

'Put it away then.'

'In a minute.'

I want to snap. No. Now. But I can't. Every sentence I say to Jake could be the last. I don't want to have a single memory of a terse word over a stupid thing like a mobile phone, or an uneaten vegetable or YouTube.

22:22

'I think we should bed down, don't you?'

'Yeah, chilly now innit?'

'Isn't it.'

'What?'

'Doesn't matter. Love you, Jake.'

'Love you too, Mum.'

22:37

Laid out straight like a corpse in a coffin, I wonder how Dave had even fit in the tent. Jake must be more comfortable than me; he has switched into standby mode. I try to mimic his position but my extra height, for which I am usually grateful, stops me straightening my legs. I end up with a pain in my lower back or my neck or my knees depending on the way I curl into the space. I roll over and lift one knee, forming the shape of a chalked-outline of a dead body. Not comfortable either. On my stomach I straighten out and start to count the stitching around the seams of the tent. Too difficult. I move on to counting the waves pounding on the pebbly shore of Warden Point, making me think of the sleeping fossils we might uncover tomorrow. I feel awake enough to manage without my emergency supplies but pat my coat pocket to check they're still there.

Whilst Jake packed his rucksack, I had nipped out to the shop. The shady guy, who waits near the trolleys outside Iceland, is always passing something to someone and it didn't hurt to ask if he had something that might help me. I waited until the carpark was as clear as possible and checked over my shoulder, twice, before approaching him.

Have you got something that will keep me awake? He looked me up and down, no doubt judging my cagoule and memory-foam Skechers combo. He waited for several moments before speaking, scanning the shoppers loading their car boots and fiddling with change to find a suitable coin for their trolley. Once he was satisfied with his surveillance, he looked down and spoke to the floor. *You're new.*

Yeah, first time. I need something to keep me awake.

That rave on the beach?

I laughed nervously. *No but I do need to stay awake tonight.*
He put his hand into his over-the-shoulder bag. The Adidas
stripes glinted under the fluorescent lights. He pulled
something out. I couldn't see it but felt it appear in the palm of
my hand. He closed my fingers around the plastic bag. His
rough skin scratching at mine. *Twenty-five quid. Rub it in your
gums. It'll take 20 minutes to hit properly.* I fumbled with my
purse and pulled out three tens. I shoved them into his hands.
Thanks. Not waiting for my change, I dashed straight back to
the car and drove round to Tesco instead, in case anyone in
Iceland had seen me talking to him.

I pull out the bag and slide the powder between my fingers.
Should I? A small amount tonight will guarantee I'm alert.
Awake might not be enough. I lick my finger and dab it in the
bag and then onto my gums, rubbing until it dissolves. The
sourness making me push my tongue into the roof of my
mouth. I lean over and hide the tiny ziplock bag at the bottom
of my rucksack and return to counting each stitch, embracing
the challenge.

5 Days

Our sleeping bags whisper to each other as the silky fabrics collide. Due to the chill in the air, I chose to stay fully clothed inside my bag. Stripping off and replacing my warm leggings and hoodie with cold pyjamas was a no from me. Even though Jake claimed I would be warmer without my layers, I couldn't bear to undress. I pull my bobble hat further over my ears. The one I don't usually get out of the basket at the back of the coat cupboard until January. My nose might also be running but I'm not sure. It's possible, it's just icy cold. 'Mum, you look like you're camping in the Arctic.'

'It feels like I am.'

'It's the beginning of October and it's mild. And it's Sheppey.'

'I know. I know. But I also know I'm freezing.' I lean in and my nose touches his cheek as I blow raspberries on his face. Heat radiates from him. I take both of his hands in mine and pull them to my face until they warm my skin. Jake goes quiet and lets me maul him with my icy fingers. His gaze bores into me. I look away and put my hands back in my sleeping bag. Self-conscious under his quiet contemplation. The wind careens across the edge of the cliff and whips the side of the tent, filling the silence between us.

'Mum, is everything okay?'

'Yeah, yeah. Course. Why do you ask?'

'I just mean with Dad and school and everything?'

'Everything's fine. We're having a little holiday. And it's good isn't it? You're enjoying it?'

'Yeah, yeah.'

'Good. Keep your hands in your sleeping bag. Keep warm.' He snuggles down further towards the end of the bag and tightens the drawstring around the hood, forming a chrysalis. Five days until his birthday. Five days until he will emerge on the other side of the line I've drawn inside my head. In some cultures twelve would be considered adulthood, wouldn't it? Don't the Native Americans send their eleven-year-old boys into the forest for three months of solitude? If they make it back, if they survive, then they are considered men. Well, they used to do that. Probably not anymore.

Staying awake is never a problem for me but being alert is. I need to be vigilant. What if the one time I must focus, I can't. What if someone comes up to the tent? The campsite owners. Malcolm. Dave. The convict roaming the island. I'd forgotten about him. He'd be trying to reach the mainland, wouldn't he? This part of Sheppey wouldn't be somewhere a convict would go, would it? I must stay alert.

If both of us are sleeping, eyes and minds closed to the world, we are vulnerable. Why do humans sleep for such long periods of time? At least when animals hibernate, they build a nest and hide. Humans lie in the open. Adrift. Waiting for something to happen to them. If you hide, you're safe.

Jake's snuffling settles into long, slow breaths. His bottom lip hangs open. He's out. Riding the deep sleep wave.

I roll over and pull the bag out of the bottom of my rucksack, lick my index finger and poke at the contents. Sherbet Fountains were my childhood favourite and a stick of liquorice to chew on now wouldn't go amiss. The powder lacks the sweetness of sherbet and has its own uniquely sour tang. I rub it into my gums trying to avoid my taste buds as I repeat the process. Is there a correct dose? I need to be ultra-alert so go for one more application. I close the bag, hide it again and wait.

Its bitter taste lingers in my mouth. An occasional piece of grit catching between my teeth and releasing another sour hit. I need a drink. I lean to the edge of the tent, grab Jake's unfinished Dr Pepper and take a swig. With no fizz left, the syrup clings to the plaque on my teeth but least it's sweet.

I try tilting my head to and fro. The drugs are working. The usual sluggishness resting inside me isn't there. The usual sense of exhaustion keeping me horizontal is long gone. I clearly didn't take enough last night, because every atom in my body now pops around inside me saying, get up, move, jump. You can do anything. I can't lean on the wall of the tent to read so instead I flip over in my sleeping bag, like a clumsy mermaid, and lean on my elbows. I balance the torch on my pillow and open *The Bell Jar*.

Midnight approaches and I continue to read by torch light, spinning over every twenty minutes or so to relieve the ache building up in my neck and hip. Switching hands and elbows each time.

My feet and legs feel jumpy. Not pins and needles but a strange sensation that I want to shake out of them. I wriggle from inside the sleeping bag, aware I risk releasing all my accumulated heat — although the aching cold of earlier has passed, perhaps a bonus side effect of the drugs. As my feet take the weight of my bent-over body, the strange fuzzy sensation travelling up to my hips eases a little. Putting my hands out in front of me, I crawl from the tent on all fours, manipulating the zip under my thumb to keep its roar as quiet as possible.

The night sky blinks with stars. Thousands of them. I shake out my legs and keep my arms wrapped closely around my body. I jump up and down a few times and the weird sensation pounding in my veins starts to dissipate. A few steps across the field might help my muscles relax. Walking towards the boundary, I count my footsteps and hold my arms out as if I am flying. The night sky absorbs me in its abyss.

One hundred and fifty steps to the edge. In the distance, the tent stands out: a small green dome. The door flaps in the wind coming off the sea. I turn back to the coastline and watch the foam floating atop the lapping waves, catching the edge of the moonlight. I admire the vast universe, wide enough to swallow me whole. Or Jake. If he were absent from my life, a great chasm would open inside me. An unfillable one. My eyes pivot to the tent. It looks insignificant under the frame of the sky. I count my steps as I return to Jake.

Once back in my sleeping bag, I pick my book up and carry on reading. I try again to lean on the wall of the tent, but despite pulling taut, the canvas does not have the stability to take my weight.

The pins and needles in my limbs pass but fogginess starts to gather inside my head. Soon I lose focus and my body, heavy and drained, pulls me into the hard floor. My vision narrows and darkens, making me realise my eyes might be swollen. I'm drowsy. Are the drugs wearing off? I need to stay awake all night. The bag has some more in but I wanted to save it for tomorrow. Maybe it is more important I stay awake tonight. Deal with tomorrow, tomorrow.

I pull it out. A flutter of white follows and I remember the soft talcum powder I shook over Jake's bathed baby body, the silky texture of his infant skin. I lick my finger and gather up the dust. Some clings to my nail while other stray particles settle on my ring.

I bought the ring before my amniocentesis test. I flicked aimlessly through a catalogue trying to distract myself from the thoughts of miscarriages and malformed foetuses, and the modern silver band inset with an oval green stone took me by surprise. Strong and simple. I looked at the description and price and found that the jewellery collection was called Hope. So apt. I ordered the ring and wore it every day as a reminder to myself that I would never be without hope. Once his test results confirmed there were no extra chromosomes it became a good luck charm. I never take it off, not even now that the silver setting has chunks missing, damaged when I caught it on a door handle. *You're too superstitious, Viv.* Dave never understood me. I lick the residue from my ring and push the bag back into my rucksack.

4 Days

20:16

From the door of the tent, I keep my eye on Jake as he wiggles his hips and splashes pee over the hedgerows. Once he was far enough away not to see, I rushed to scavenge the remnants of my party drug from the creases of the bag, licking and dipping and stroking the last hit onto my gums. As Jake starts his walk back to the tent, I settle back inside and busy myself by sweeping the damp sand from the floor with the palms of my hands.

'Shoes!' My voice comes out in a squeak. I cough until my throat clears.

'Shake off your shoes before you come in.' While Jake smashes the soles of his trainers together, scattering more damp sand into the air, I repeat the sweeping motion again and again. 'Away from the door, Jake. I'm trying to get rid of the sand, not add to it.'

'Sorry, Mum.' He stands, gazing through the entrance at my

frantic tidying. 'When are we going home?'

'Why?' I stop. Straining my neck to look up at him. 'You not enjoying yourself?'

'Yeah, I am. It's just—'

'What? This is what we needed, don't you think?'

'Yeah, I guess.' He looks away from me. Towards the farm beyond the pond and then back towards the shoulder of the cliff and the sea.

'I sense a but coming.'

'Well, my phone is dead.'

'You'll survive without your phone. This trip is about life without technology. It's about survival.' My words tumble out. My tongue has a life and pace of its own.

Jake scans the tent and screws up his nose.

'Hardly, Mum. We've got multi-packs of crisps, Mint Imperials, peanut M&Ms and a gas stove. It doesn't matter, I only wondered, that's all.'

'Couple more days, okay? So we can relax properly.' I straighten out the sleeping bags and re-stack the mini-boxes of cereals that we'll be eating dry tomorrow as we've finished the milk.

'You don't seem relaxed.'

'Don't I?' My words race out my mouth. My breath quickens. I try to slow myself down. To fake nonchalance. 'Well, I am Jake. Tot-all-y re-lax-ed.' My attempt at mimicking the

Caribbean drawl from the Lilt adverts of my childhood, makes me sound like a broken cassette tape with a tangled and twisted ribbon. The kettle whistles. 'Come on in here and let's eat.'

We tear off the foil lids from the Pot Noodles and pour the water in. 'I got the branded ones you like, no Iceland specials tonight!' I pass Jake a fork. 'Stir it. And don't burn your mouth.' We zip up the door to block out the wind. The sound of our breathing, as we blow cooling air over each mouthful, fills the tent along with the slurp of noodles being sucked between lips. The smell of synthetic chow mein lingers, clinging to the canvas.

'Can we go home tonight to charge our phones and then come back out?'

'Really? You're that desperate to charge your phone?'

'Well, yeah.'

'Err. No. It's not a technology break if you pop home to recharge. And this proves you need one.'

'But I don't want a technology break.'

'But I do. For both of us.' He leans across me and the teeth of the tent's zip cuts the tension. 'Where are you going?'

'To the loo.'

'Again?'

'I think I need a number two now, if you must know.'

'Oh lovely! Well, take some loo roll and a bag then. Don't dilly-dally.' I pass him an empty crisp packet. 'Put it in this and then take it straight to the bin.'

'Urghh—'

'Mind your drink. You're so clumsy. When did your feet start to resemble boats? When did you get so big?' I want to smile, but the thought of him growing frightens it away. He's so close to twelve. I stare at his half-empty can. Jake wants to go home. Will he leave without me? The tone of his voice, scratchy and harsh, frightens me.

'Off you go then.'

The tent door flaps. Why, when he's ill, did I drag him out to the cliff top where there are no toilets? Where there's nothing sanitary at all. I look up and the tent starts to spin.

'Focus, Vivian. Focus.' My own voice echoes around the tent. I fish in my pocket and pull out the bag of drugs. It is empty but for an odd white speck clinging to the seam of the zip seal. How can I be vigilant enough, alert enough, without something to focus my mind? What if tonight the escaped convict prowls these cliffs? Although the chance of sleep remains slim, I need to be alert to protect him. Awake is not enough.

If I can't be on high alert maybe there's another way. I can make sure that Jake can't leave. I stuff the bag to the bottom of my rucksack and feel around for the hard plastic of my pill bottle. My blue pills. I could crack a capsule into Jake's Dr Pepper. Half a dose would be okay. He's nearly twelve, even if he is so slim that when we were fossil hunting earlier this morning it looked like the sea wind would lift him off the shore. Before anyone else was out of bed, we had trekked along the beach. He hadn't complained about his lack of phone while we watched the sunrise, our backs against the remnants of the concrete World War II pillbox.

I prise open the capsule, aiming the powdered sleep into the small gap in the can. I swill the liquid around and place it back where he left it. I dump the blue plastic casing in the bottom of my empty noodle pot and sit back, relieved that Jake won't be going anywhere tonight.

21:37

'Finish your Dr Pepper before you clean your teeth.' I pass him the can.

'It tastes a bit weird.'

'Probably the fifty Mint Imperials you've munched through. Drink up. I want to be snuggled up by ten.' He tips his head back and empties the can.

22:59

After last night's session, I have a couple of chapters of my book remaining and as I finish the last page, I can't shake off a strange sensation creeping across my body. Diaphanous. Where did that word come from? My limbs are translucent. I can see through my flesh to the ground underneath. My arms and legs are solid under my hands but my head sees things that aren't there. Am I like Esther in my book? Am I unstable? It doesn't matter. I need to focus on Jake.

Jake's deep sleep and the shadows cast by my torch make him look cadaverous. The ivory tone of his skin has swallowed his freckles. There is a blue tinge to his lips. I can't hear him breathing. I struggle to free myself from my sleeping bag. Have I overdosed him on my medication? I can't have done. He's not twelve for another four days.

I should've taken him home.

'Shit.'

I kick harder at the base of the sleeping bag and break free. Taking my fingers out of my gloves, I place them on his neck. The dampness of his warmth highlights how cold my skinny fingers are. My rings spin upside down; the stones dig into my palm. His pulse bounces back onto my fingertips and I close my eyes.

'Thank you, Dad.' My eyes tilt skyward. 'Thank you.'

I turn off the torch to extinguish the shadows and try to push away thoughts of corpses and autopsies. Do sleeping tablets show up in the bloodstream days, weeks or months after you've taken them? If something does happen, will they know I drugged him? I shake away the image of his still body.

The metal gurney surrounded by scalpels, callipers and weighing scales. Doctors in forensic suits lifting bloody organs and examining the digested Pot Noodle. The smell of chow mein masked by the antiseptic stench of the morgue.

23:19

From my cocooned position in my sleeping bag, I rub my feet together to create warmth. Trying to focus on the movement of each molecule and atom banging against one another, I increase the intensity of my movements. I'm so close to Jake I can feel the moisture of his breath; smell his digesting dinner mingling with minty toothpaste. His motionless face draws me in. My mind terrorises me with possibilities. I close my eyelids to shut them out but my mind ticks like a clock.

He's asleep. I don't need to be awake tonight. He won't get up in the night. I can tell by the stillness of his body, the shallowness of his breath, the tablet is working. He's safe.

I reach over to my rucksack and take out three blue tablets. I have no energy to move to the other side of the tent and find what is left of our water. I swallow them dry. Each tablet tugging as it passes down my oesophagus.

I need to cancel out the white specks I rubbed in my gums. I tip the bottle again and take a fourth, rolling and massaging my tongue around my mouth to stimulate enough saliva production so that the tablet won't stick in my throat. I lie back down, link my arms around Jake and thread my fingers through his. I wait for the drugs to work.

3 Days

A fast drum and bass beat reverberates along the beach, traversing the cliffs, reaching over to the grassy ledge and our tent. Its synthesized sounds fight with the crashing pound of waves. The man from outside Iceland thought I would use his powder to party and dance. Is it that rave starting on the coast that I can hear or is it the clubhouse at the caravan park? If I stroll down to the beach, will I find him and be able to buy some more? I need to stay awake tonight too. It is so close to Jake's birthday and I don't have much longer to save him. And I don't want to drug him again. He seemed agitated when he woke. Out of kilter. He rose at least an hour later than usual, as I suspected he would, but this change in his routine spooked him. He's such a creature of habit. He had complained of a stabbing pain behind both his eyes. *My head hurts, Mum.* He pinched his nose. *Probably the way you slept or something. Do you want some paracetamol?* I wanted to assume his headache was caused by the sleeping tablets, but I know it could be a symptom of something else. Why wouldn't he take something? I wanted him to allow me to ease his pain; the headache was my fault. He never wants painkillers; he always wants an explanation for the pain. Not for it to disappear without a trace but for it to be explained away. This time, he clung to his own diagnosis of a combination of sunstroke, windburn and a potentially iffy batch of Pot Noodle. After a session in food tech where they preached about the evils of monosodium glutamates, he started to blame my lazy food choices for his ailments. He must be feeling better though; he hasn't mentioned any aches or pains since lunch.

'How are you feeling now?'

'Good. Not so groggy.'

'I said you would feel better soon.'

'Mum, are you sure we can't go home tonight?'

'We can't. Did you know the sea air is restorative? The Victorians swore by it.'

'I think I need my bed, that's all. My brain felt so...foggy this morning, you know? I felt rubbish.'

'One more day. And talking of rubbish, would you take our bag down to the bins on the coastal path.'

'Can I test the theory of centripetal force?'

'What?'

'I'll show you.'

Jake walks to the bin swinging the carrier bag in a circular motion, turning his arm in a wide arc to test the science of the theory. He's more likely to be a science teacher than me. My son, growing and developing and learning in front of my eyes. Jake's arm drops and his eyes follow the empty Dr Pepper can and a Pot Noodle cup as they comply with scientific theory and fall, his momentum no longer smooth enough for inertia to keep it in the bag. A Tesco Bag for Life that I shouldn't be throwing away. I'm surprised Jake, the eco-warrior, hasn't mentioned my wastefulness. He'd fought for recycling bins in the playground along with the rest of the school council. The head teacher gave him a badge to wear. He stoops down and picks up the litter. It must have spread out as he has to drop to his knees to start gathering the scattered rubbish. He turns back to look at me. I wave. His eyes fall on the stray litter. He scoops it back into the noodle cup before returning it to the bag and standing up, scrunching the top of the carrier closed. He disappears from my sightline for a moment, as he makes his way to the concrete bin.

18:09

Jake keeps moving things in and around the tent. He's avoiding my gaze and speaking even less than usual. I want to ask if he's okay, but he'll ask to go home for sure. I don't want to say no to him again and saying yes isn't an option. 'Can I take a walk, Mum?'

'Where?'

'Back down the path over the fields. I won't go as far as the crumbly cliffs or the beach. I swear.' He lifts his hand to his head, holding up three fingers for the Scout promise.

'I'll come with you.'

'No. I mean, can't I go on my own for a bit? All my mates play out on their own. My headache's come back...I won't be long.'

'But—'

'Please, Mum.'

There is no one here and I know the path around the field is perfectly safe. We've walked it together several times. I search for a valid reason to refuse his request. The escaped convict would support my argument but telling him would scare him, make him want to go home even more. He must be off the island by now, or caught and back in custody.

Three more days until he's twelve. It's not more than a ten-minute walk.

'Straight there and back. It's nearly dark.'

'Well, can I have a few minutes, to, you know, watch the sheep or something?'

'Okay but not long. You've no phone remember.'

'Deal.' He scampers off before I can change my mind.

18:16

He walks away slowly and confidently, embracing his freedom. His distinctive gait is beginning to remind me of Dave's walk. The placement of his feet. The rhythm of his arms. I wish it didn't. Looking at my watch, I note the time and try to think about something else until he gets back.

18:22

Jake's probably half-way by now. He'll be standing on the far edge of the field, maybe watching the sheep graze. Trying to coax one over with a blade of grass. Or sat on the boundary fence so he can catch a glimpse of the sea over the hedgerows.

The tide is brushing over the beach, reaching the pillbox. Each wave biting at the concrete, eroding its sharp edges. Seaweed will rush in and out as it clings to the barnacled surface. Its tendrils twirling with the tide. He promised not to go down to the sea, to stay at the edge of the farmer's land but the path to the beach does lead off the field.

He wouldn't.

My eyes stay on the neat line of the horizon where the edge of the cliff meets the sea. Jake will reappear here, emerging head first from the ocean like Poseidon.

18:26

He's been gone ten minutes. His head should appear soon. Sand martins or maybe swallows swoop up and down the cliffs, chasing each other. I can hear them but I daren't turn to watch the last of their show for fear of missing Jake's return.

18:29

I begin to pace. Reluctant to go after him as I'd promised him some space. I remind myself I trust him. I do. When he was younger, after watching some eighties kids' film we started to pretend to spit in our hands and shake on our promises. Was it *The Goonies* we copied it from? A tradition we never dropped. *I swear I will clean my room. I swear I brushed my teeth. I swear to love you forever.* At least I would not be breaking one of our pacts if I went after him. He normally instigated the sacred handshake but tonight he hadn't. Did he intend to break his promise?

Where is he?

18:31

My pace quickens as I circle the perimeter of our camp. My strides become deeper; my circle wider. I trust Jake but I don't trust anyone else.

18:33

He should be back by now or at least on his way. I will go to the edge and watch him appear. I will call out and tell him to hurry because his hot chocolate will be ready soon.

Have I left the kettle on the stove unattended?

My feet accelerate as I consider all the possible accidents Jake could have had. How stupid I have been. The tragedy won't happen on a school trip but here, on the island of his birth, camping with me. I'll be the mother whose toddler drowned in their garden pond. The mother whose child died because she left his inhaler at home. The mother whose child was abducted on her watch.

I sprint towards the fields.

18:37

I reach the fork in the path. My hands drop to my knees as I catch my breath. The long swaying grasses, along with the gradient of the cliff, block my view. He shouldn't be down there. He should be across the field but it's empty and he isn't climbing upwards on the cliff trail either. I look behind me. Still no one. He must have decided to go to the beach despite his promise. I begin the descent. My feet whirl under me. The steepness lending me speed as the path zig-zags its way down the side of the cliff. Still no sign of Jake. Is his black hoodie disguised by the falling dusk?

I skid to a stop as I reach the bottom. The whole beach and its parallel path are empty. A speck in the distance starts to emerge from a rising mist. A dog walker? A mile away at best.

'Jake!'

Louder. 'Jake!'

The ocean calls back to me with empty groans.

18:57

Irrational thoughts sink from my head to my stomach like stones, pinning me to the spot. Has he fallen in the sea? He wouldn't be that stupid. That careless. 'Trust him, Vivian.'

He is sensible.

But what about strangers. Convicts. Overly familiar neighbours.

The shingle shrinks until the scrimshaw fragments, sharp between my bare feet, get sucked into the neaping tide. I run to the pill box and check all four sides, even scrambling through the knee-deep water to reach the top so I can check the insides. I leave the skin from my knee behind.

I throw myself from the top and land on all fours. Salt water stings my fresh graze, but I don't register the pain. I brush silt from my hands. Grains stubbornly cling between each finger and refuse to let go.

Back on the promenade, I try to focus on the vast empty sea in front of me. There are no boats or buoys. A flat grey expanse stretches outwards, with barely a ripple in sight.

Caws of sea birds fight to be heard over a primal screech that surges towards the shallows. I feel the burn in my throat as I let it go.

A rabbit appears at the base of the cliff. Its eyes glint, red and sharp. It disappears into the marram grass. I follow.

I walk now, unable to run up the steep gradient of the cliff path. Once at the tent, I plant myself on the floor. The kettle is off and cold. My feet are tinged blue. I dare not move away from the tent again in case he comes back. Perhaps he detoured off the path to visit the horses at the farm. Or became distracted by a stray dog or a prowling cat. If he returns and I'm not here, he'll panic. It's been over an hour. An hour is not 'don't be long'. Our dead mobiles now seem a frivolous existential crisis. Untraceable isn't the same as being uncontactable. I wrap my arms around myself and sway in time with the rhythm of the tide.

22:01

The cloudy sky masks the moon so that I can't see more than a foot ahead of me. My bare hands, pale and dry, are barely visible. The wind picks up a top layer of sandy soil and lashes it against the tent, the canvas walls heave as if breathing. When the wind changes direction, the material buffets, pulling at the tent pegs in the earth. Are they secure enough to prevent the tent from being whipped off the cliff? Dorothy's house, ripped from its ranch, spiralling through the Kansas sky, petrified me as a child.

Has Jake gone home? Like Dorothy wanted to.

Jake's rucksack leans into the corner of the tent and makes me think of Dave. It once belonged to him. Went with him on his fishing weekends. When he needed space. Did Jake need space? Did he go home? The walk would take an hour at most. If he didn't get lost. I can't think about his dubious sense of direction now. He knows the spare key sits beneath the ceramic yellow wellies by the back door, where trailing succulents burst from their tops. Surely, the desire to charge his phone wouldn't push him to do something so reckless, so thoughtless. He would know that my tongue would be swelling now, my temples pulsing, a vice-like pressure crushing my sinuses. He'd witnessed my panic attacks when Dave left. Eased me out of the other side of more than one. Alternative scenarios race in front of my eyes.

Accidents.

A coma. On his birthday, they'll have to turn off life support. Dying on his birthday like Shakespeare.

Three hours. If I called the police, or Dave, they would ask too many questions. *Why are you camping? Why isn't he in France or at school?* Anyway, my phone is flat.

Would he have gone to a friend's to charge his phone? Surely not, at this time of night. He would be too embarrassed to explain how and why he'd ended up on their doorstep.

An owl hoots across the field, searching for its prey.

My lips crack and the taste of iron seeps into my mouth. They stick together as I try to part them with my sandpaper tongue. I feel sick. My breath shoots from my mouth, short and shallow: an engine revving to its limits. I need a drink. The last of the water is in the kettle. I check the weight of it. Enough. I grab my plastic beaker from my bag. My pill bottle is wedged inside. Turning it upside down, I shake it free. The container tumbles across the groundsheet. I blow the dust and dry grass from the lip of the cup. I pour in the unpleasantly tepid water. Swill it around my mouth and swallow. Bits of lime scale cling to my teeth. As I take another gulp, the crack in my top lip deepens. Blood reaches into my mouth and I can taste it. The same blood that flows through Jake. Where is he? I cannot leave. What should I do?

I have no choice. I'll have to wait.

A drop of rain hits the canvas and as the timpani accelerates, it starts to batter the tent. I pull the zip closed but not before a puddle forms at my feet. I drag my fingers through it and pull droplets of water across the ground sheet. My hand stops as it collides with the plastic bottle. I hold my lifeline in my fist. It will get me through the waiting. The bottle rattles as I battle with the child lock. It fights me but I squeeze in the exact spot and it opens. I tip the contents into my cupped hand. Two blue tablets. Another flick of the wrist. Three. I peer inside. One left. I invert the bottle. Four. I'll wait here. The tablets will take the edge off my worst fears until Jake comes back. He will come back.

22:43

The rain falls in larger drops as if the sea breeze is lifting the ocean and scattering it over the island. The tent sags under the weight of the accumulating water. It's not designed for a deluge. The moisture works its way through the canvas, gravitating to the seams and adding to the small puddle from the open door. Something tickles at my foot and I push it away. The end of my sleeping bag squelches. I hold Jake's pillow in my arms and the empty pill bottle in the other. I toss and turn as my blue tablets fight with the remnants of the powdery wonder that lingers in my bloodstream.

I step over the railings onto the beach and wade through the advancing tide. Fossils the size of dinner plates drift past me. Seaweed and octopus tentacles wind themselves around my ankles. I pull free and move toward the pillbox. I drag myself up, impressed by the strength in my slender arms and stand atop the ruined structure. The midnight sky sparkles over the North Sea and highlights the sequins adorning the flowing train of my wedding dress. It glitters. A ship eases past the island, making its way to the dockyard. Sailors wave from the deck. I guard my eyes from the blinding moonlight, like a cartoon sailor scanning the horizon for pirates. Jake stands up in the distance, as if walking on water, balancing as the water ebbs and flows. He waves back this time. I can see the rowing boat under his feet now, moving away from me. The tide aids his escape; the current maximising his momentum. The water at my feet swells with the wake from his boat and expands in size with each return motion until the ebb of the tide reaches my waist, then my breasts. My nipples harden. Salt water stings my eyes and smarts as it enters the cut on my lip. My tongue stretches out of my mouth to salve the wound. A final wave pounds my chest so fiercely I am knocked off the pillbox and deposited in the sea. My dress billows around me. I can no longer stand up and hold my head above the water. The waves pull me back and forth, smashing me against the concrete. Water fills my mouth. I gasp for air.

I bolt upright. Awake.

I suck in the stale tent air, my chest burning with the pressure to breathe. I kick and shove and scramble my way out of my sleeping bag. My fingers are so cold and wet they can't grasp the zip. Fatigue weakens them further. Where am I? The rain claws at the canvas walls. I am in a tent. My hands are damp from the water on the floor. I wriggle back, away from the door. I re-enter the sleeping bag. Pushing into its depths. I shuffle into the far corner, away from the encroaching water, to an area kept dry by the slight incline of the cliff. I start to shake.

23:01

The rain sounds like voices. The wind, footsteps. My head lolls under its own weight. Pressed into the floor of the tent, the imprint of the groundsheet leaves marks on my cheeks. My sallow, clammy skin wrinkled and wet.

The zip unfurls, like the sound of Concorde lifting off. I groan as the noise scrapes at my skull. I cannot lift the foggy lump of my head to see who is opening the tent. Is it Jake? Blood blossoms on my re-cracked lip as I stretch my mouth to speak. *Jake?* No words form. An animal cry escapes instead.

'Vivian?'

A large head with a mane of hair, connected to a wiry beard, peers through the gap. Malcolm? I push myself further into the corner. The canvas straining with the curve of my back. The man's green uniform blends with the walls of the tent. I try to focus on his eyes, but his thick eyebrows keep moving like eels. Another voice calls out. I let my head fall again and feel water on my face. The man is trying to get into our small two-man tent, kneeling on me in the process. I scream but I am not sure any sound comes out. A satisfying swoosh of fabric being sliced by a blade follows and the canvas ceiling drops like a waterfall. The rain falls on my face. Already wet, I am now saturated, as if I swam across the ocean. I'm weightless. I'm strapped down and moving across the land. Someone is taking me somewhere. Is this the end? Is it me who doesn't see Jake live past twelve? Did he get it wrong? My body jumps and jolts as we traverse the potholed path off the campsite. A heavy blanket presses down on my skin. Pulsing blue lights flash behind my eyelids. Doors slam. Sirens sound in the distance.

2 Days

I can hear Jake and Dave at my bedside. The dark night bleeds into the room through the undressed windows. Their words drift through the air and into my mind. Jake holds my hand tightly, cutting off the circulation to my fingertips until they must be the colour of cherry blossom, chalky with pink edges.

'She'll wake, Jake. Don't worry. Her body is just recovering from the stress and the cold.'

'You saved her, son. Remember that. We are so proud of you.'

My eyelids flutter when they speak. Scabs cover the cracks at the edge of my lips so Jake dabs at them with a sponge and ice chips. It tastes like sea mist. He massages my hands and feet with a silky hand cream, releasing the scent of peonies and roses. His small fingers trace each of my knuckles as he gently circles the cream into my fractured skin, avoiding the cannula in the back of my hand. The scent reminds me of summer flowers, but cannot cover the antiseptic scent of the ward or the over-stewed vegetables they must be serving patients, not that I've had anything to eat. There are knocks and bangs as Jake tidies my bedside table but I still cannot open my eyes.

'I bought you some Galaxy, Mum. The sharing size.' He squeezes my hand every time he speaks. Is he smiling? 'And Leanne brought you grapes.'

Someone stands. The shadow blocks out the fluorescent lights above me. 'Come on. Time to go.' Dave.

'Bye, Mum.' Jake arranges my hands together on my lap and I feel the trail of his fingertips reach my toes as he leaves.

1 Day

21:31

Jake's in my arms. Each small finger attempting to grip one of mine. The pearly fingernails are delicate and tiny, but sharp as broken glass. His tufts of black hair stick up in varying directions, still damp from the amniotic fluid. There is no flow or rhythm to its shape. His lips and skin are so soft under my own fingertips that I can barely feel them.

My uncle, who died years ago, stands beside me. My father beams with pride. My grandparents, also dead, form a queue across the room, waiting to get a look at their great grandson. They look too fragile to hold him so I pull him in closer to my chest. I smother him between my swollen breasts.

You must let him breathe. My father tugs gently on my sleeve. I release my grip a little.

The sound of the ocean whispers as my grandparents gather around. They stroke his miniscule ears and nose with their wrinkled, liver-spotted hands. Their fingernails are yellow and brittle with age. The ocean waves start to pound harder, crashing. The pressure builds in my eardrums, my sinuses. I let Jake go and pinch at the bridge of my nose. My maternal grandmother catches him.

No. He's mine, I cry. *He's mine.*

The squealing beeps of a monitor blend into one continuous tone.

21:37

A shadow returns. A female voice, not Dave nor Jake. It must be a nurse who holds my hand as she administers something through my cannula. A cold trickle passes through my veins. Travelling up my wrist. 'She's stable now, but call the family,' says another voice. 'Tell them to come back. Just in case.'

Jake's Birthday

14:00

Jake stands at my bedside. The overpowering smell of Lynx Africa telling me if he hasn't washed he has at least thought about it. The tearing of paper roars near my ears. He must be opening the cards he has brought with him. He reads aloud. 'Wishing you a speedy recovery. All the best. Leanne and Hugh. Grandma sent a text and says she's on the next flight home when she docks in Athens.' He strokes my still hand in his. I want to squeeze it but the instruction is not making it to my fingers.

I can smell Dave too. His deodorant is muskier than Jake's. He holds something over me, the paper rustles. 'Malcolm sent you these. I think they're pink carnations, with some tiny white buds too.' An unfamiliar voice adds, 'Gypsophila.'

'Put them on here, Dad, so she can smell them.' Jake moves things around. A crinkle of chocolate foil. Has he eaten his gift without me? 'Malcolm's card says, get well soon. And Smudge says he misses you too.' My eyelids flutter. Light and shade flashing through them. Jake holds my hands tighter. His are warm and soft, mine are dry. I wish he would massage in that cream again. It smelt pretty. The hospital lights glare down on my head, blurring everything to starchy white. I can see the tubes in my veins out of the corner of my eye. Violet ribbons carrying my blood. The skin on my arms alabaster white. Strands of limp hair cling to my face. I can't reposition myself so that I can see more but I try. My body is a fossilised shell, immobile.

'Come on, Jake. Let's grab a cuppa and let her sleep.'

I'm not sleeping, I want to say.

Jake's head looks from me to Dave. I can see the edge of it turn.

'I'll get you a Twix. It's your birthday, after all'. Dave laughs. 'Come on. She'll be okay.'

He's made it to twelve. I put all my energy into my eyes. Making the sclera bulge. Pushing each eyelash towards my brow. Come on! Open!

The white light blinds me. I shut them again. I try a little slower. Try to focus on the body shapes. Jake is still holding my fingers. Dave, the shadow near the door, tugging on his other hand. I blink. Refocus again. Jake is looking towards his dad, allowing himself to be pulled away. But he holds on to my fingers. He lets his body be dragged into the shape of a crucifix, one fingertip touching my damp skin and the other entering the hospital corridor with his father. We disconnect. My strength reaches from my eyes to my fingertips in time for me to clench the shadow of Jake's hand. Their footsteps chime a rhythm that echoes in the sterile room.

Desperate, I redirect my energy to my voice. I must catch him before he leaves. The first noise, a grunt, barely makes it to my lips. I try again. Pulling my vocal chords tight. Swallowing back fear and the pain caused by my unanswered screams. In my head, I chant his name.

Jake. Jake. Jake.

The primal noise misses the initial sound.

'...ake.'

The footsteps stop. My eyes are open. His rubber soles squeak as he pivots on the tile floor.

'Mum!'

Jake races to my side. This time I manage the whole word.

'Dad, quick! Mum's awake! She's okay!'

'Jake.' He swallows me in his arms. He feels stronger and larger than ever as he holds my body in his.

+84 Days

Average sleep 5 hours 17 minutes

My doctor claims my steady recovery shows progress. Today she signed me off for a final fortnight. I've been weaned off the sleeping tablets, and restrict my use to the herbal ones now, and only if things start to overwhelm me. Mum paid for a weekly one to one counsellor and those sessions ended three weeks ago but I haven't fallen to pieces. The steps to happiness have helped me find meaning in my days. And the HRT's helping!

We spread dad's ashes over the beach yesterday. Jake, Mum and I and then Dave came too. I told him he didn't have to, and I meant it but he realises now that Jake needs him even when his grunts suggest otherwise. The sun came out as we let the ashes fall into the breaking waves and we stayed for long enough to make us think spring will be upon us again soon.

Jake's second high school parent's evening went well and they were sensitive enough not to mention his attendance or when I would be back to work. Occupational health are making sure my morning only time-table will ease me back into the workplace and I've no pressure to work one on one with pupils until I'm ready. Jake remains on track to reach his grades and Malcolm has been tutoring him on Saturday mornings. After they've hit the books, they head to his workshop. I have a feeling I might be getting a new bird table soon.

Positives this week include choosing a return to work outfit (it's still from a charity shop but someone with taste and money must've had a clear out and it's greener), my daily walks along the beach bring me closer to dad — we are thinking of getting a rescue dog to keep me company when Jake's at his dad's for the weekend. Leanne and I meet up every fortnight and we have started a book club together. Both our mums come and we are hoping to get some new members to join us soon. We have commandeered a table at the Working Mens' Club. I worry less about what tomorrow will bring. The end of the world only feels close when I stand for too long on the seafront and imagine what *SS Richard Montgomery* is doing under the water. Bedtime no longer frightens me and Jake's plans for his thirteenth birthday party are already well underway.

Acknowledgements

Where should I start? As this is my debut novel, the acknowledgements are proving difficult to write – after all I could name all my teachers, my family, my friends and my writers' groups individually. And I do thank all of those people but first I need to thank Ros Barber for allowing me to use a line from her poem as my title (the poem can be read forwards or backwards – flick back to the epigraph and try it – it's very impressive). When I entered the Bridport Prize in 2024, worrying about permissions never crossed my mind. Her generosity allowed me to use the full poem in the novel and gave me a cracking anecdote to share at any future events (you will need to attend to hear it). If you want to read more by Ros, please head to her website: www.rosbarber.com

A talented artist made this cover possible. Charlotte Packman's gorgeous painting features inside my protagonist's head (proud mum moment) and manages to demonstrate the anxiety of Vivian, and her isolation on the Isle of Sheppey, all in one image. Charlotte I hope you know you will be designing all my future book covers – and thank you for all the birthday wishes you gifted me. For more of Charlotte's art head to her Instagram page @charpackman_artanddesign. Both of us also need to thank Viv from Lucky Hare Books and Helen from Protea Press for playing around with fonts, colours and sizing until it popped.

Leon Packman, you may not have worked on the cover but without all your accidents (he really did have five ambulances before he was five), I'm not sure I would have been able to create such a believable main character. Every little worry of Vivian's is one of mine, amplified.

The first draft of this novel was conceived in 2021 for my MA dissertation. My dad, to whom this book is dedicated, was dying. Those of you who know me, know I love a self-imposed deadline. My dad was given six weeks to live and I knew I needed to finish it before he died so my dissertation plans didn't derail. My dad was my biggest fan. I finished the first draft, and my dissertation submission about ten days before he died. This book is for him.

Thanks go to anyone and everyone who read this in draft form, from a short extract on my blog to whole re-writes. To all my fellow MA graduates – when I had only written the opening chapter, you were all very opinionated about how it should end

- I hope you find it satisfying. Thank you to Karen Seager for her Sheppey sensitivity read and to Laila Trillow Editorial for post-MA feedback and to Julie Gourichas, an agent who recommended I read the comp title *Bright Burning Things* by Lisa Harding. This prompted a re-write to first person and I fell in love with my book all over again. With my confidence increased, I entered the Bridport Novel Prize 2024. Thank you to every reader/judge who nudged my entry through to the longlisting. I still have to pinch myself to believe it.

If you have ever read my blog, or shared my blog – thank you. I started blogging as the Yellow Brick Road Writer to document my journey to publication. When I started in 2022, I had no idea by November 2024 I would be founding an indie publishing company. Sophie E Mills and Helen J Worthington-Smith, I wouldn't have this book in my hands if it hadn't been for you two. The possibility for Protea Press to change the face of publishing is very real and I wouldn't want to be on this journey with anybody else.

We are getting close to the end, I promise. Claire Scarr and Emma Gibson – you two see me through the highs and lows of teaching. You have championed my writing every step of the way. My bookish weekends with you two are the best – here's to many more years at Hay Festival and all the other festivals and bookshops we visit every year. You two rock.

Some of you reading this may know me as a literary festival organiser (Ampthill Literary Festival), book club host (Ampthill Beer & Books) and interviewer (thank you for having me Lucky Hare Books, Ampthill) and I want you to know, being part of these events has enabled me to be here today, writing the acknowledgements to my debut novel. I do hope you all enjoy it.

To all my family, friends, colleagues, present and former pupils, blog readers, Ampthill Writers' Group, Writing Bedfordshire, Dr Clare Walsh and everyone who has ever cared enough to listen to me talk about my books – thank you.

The final mention must go to Doug, Charlotte, Leon and my mum. You may have thought I was crazy staring at my laptop day and night, and I cannot promise I will work any less now my first book is out in the world, but at least you can start telling people about my books and why I am always working.

About the Author

Kate grew up reading widely and has eclectic taste. Likewise, her work refuses to fit into a specific genre. Writing for adults and children, Kate enjoys exploring themes linked to identity, and playing with time in the structure of her novels.

Once Kate realised being an insurance broker did not meet her creative needs, she completed a BA(Hons) in English Studies. Despite being determined not to teach, she has spent the last decade teaching English in a middle school and loves it. Recently she completed an MA in Creative Writing at Birkbeck. In July 2024 she was longlisted for the Bridport Novel Prize.

When not reading or writing, she organises pop-up book clubs and hosts author events. She chaired Ampthill Literary Festival for five years.

PROTEA PRESS

A boutique publisher nurturing new talent.

Our mission is to publish excellent and original stories whilst supporting and nurturing the talent that write them. We aim to redefine independent publishing in a flexible and cooperative way, that brings authors together as a community.

Visit www.proteapress.co.uk to find out more or turn the page to see some of our other publications. All are available to buy through our website. You can also follow us at:

Linkedin: Protea Press

X: @protea_press

Instagram: proteapressbooks

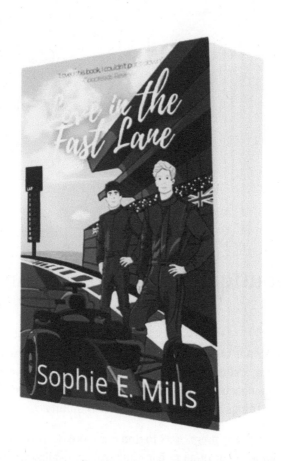

Love in the Fast Lane

Sophie E. Mills

Available to buy at <u>www.proteapress.co.uk</u>

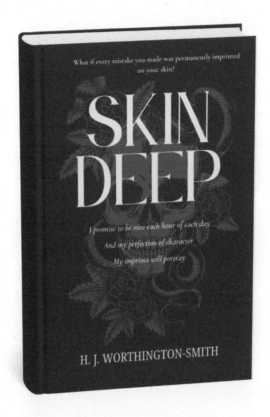

Skin Deep

H. J. Worthington-Smith

Available to buy at <u>www.proteapress.co.uk</u>

BV - #0076 - 090125 - C0 - 198/129/17 - PB - 9781917506045 - Matt Lamination